SOMETIMES...
YOU JUST HAD
TO RUN

THE
cleat
RETREAT

BEAUTY AND THE CLEATS PREQUEL

KRIS BUTLER

The Cleat Retreat
A Beauty and the Cleats Prequel
Kris Butler

First Edition: August 2023
Published by: Incognito Scribe Productions LLC
Copyright © Kris Butler 2023

Proofreading: © 2023 by Owlsome Author Services
Formatting: © 2023 Incognito Scribe Productions LLC
Photo Credit: © 2023 Emma Jane Photography
Model Credit: © 2023 Kaylee Garber
Cover Design: © 2023 Incognito Scribe Productions LLC

❀ Created with Vellum

THE
cleat
RETREAT
A BEAUTY AND THE CLEATS PREQUEL
KRIS BUTLER

CONTENTS

BLURB

The only thing worse than almost dying as a child... surviving.

Now, hear me out. I was very much happy to be alive. It was the constant need to feel grateful for something I had no control over... that grated on me.

I'd become so passive in my own life that when my boyfriend proposed, I couldn't remember what I liked about him outside of his dimple. I mean, it was cute. But enough to marry someone? Nah.

I hadn't meant to be a runaway bride, but here I was, all dressed in white and escaping the baseball diamond like my life depended on it. Just a good old cleat retreat.

Landing in my brother's best friend's car was a nice surprise. Spending the next twenty-four hours with him…even better. Maybe I could convince him to rid me of my pesky virginity once and for all. Besides, I knew the score, and he never played for keeps. He was the one who'd coined the term cleat retreat in the first place.

A virginal bride and a grumpy tatted baseball player sharing one bed. What could possibly go wrong?

Join the players of the Blue Devils and the Yellowjackets as they play the game of love and baseball. This is an interconnected standalone series, meaning the books can be read in any order. These books will consist of why-choose, menage, and MM. Please check the foreward of each book for list of triggers and content.

The Cleat Retreat: Blake's prequel (Best read before Pitch Slap)
The Pitch Slap: Blake's story (Why-choose)
No Balking Way: Bryce's story (ménage)
Whiff it Real Good: Ledger's story (MM)

FOREWORD

This book has sexual scenes meant for adults. It is a why-choose romance, and this book will introduce the love interests, but will only be MF on page. The steamy scenes are steamy, and you might need new batteries by the end. Sorry, not sorry. This book uses the F-word as well as other foul language.

TROPES AND CONTENT

- Multi-Pov
- Praise
- Possessive, growly men
- Runaway bride
- Virgin's first time
- Brother's Best Friend
- Baseball
- Tattoos

- Partial skinny dipping

SENSITIVE TOPICS

- 'God, Jesus, Hell, Damn' used casually or in a sexual context
- PTSD/panic attacks
- Medical illness/history
- Controlling parents
- Depression/anxiety
- Cliffhanger (Prequel leads into next book)

It's never too late to figure out who you are and make your own path.

Blake

ONE

I OFTEN HAD A RECURRING nightmare where I would find myself standing in the center of a crowd with everyone's focus on me. The venue differed each time, but no matter where I was, from an opera house to the pitcher's mound, the rest was always the same.

I'd be surrounded by people—some familiar, some strangers—as they urged me to do… *something*. It was the "something" I could never figure out and would send me into a frenzy.

I'd stand there frozen, zooming from one face to the next as they waited for me. With each face I peered at, I hoped to discover the secret of what I needed to do. That someone would give me a clue on how to make the staring stop.

I really needed the staring to stop.

The longer I felt their stares, the more I panicked. My heart would speed up, my skin would flush, and ̶̶̶̶̶̶̶̶̶ telltale signs of sweat as it beaded beneath my shirt. My breath would become shallow as I continued to search the crowd for someone to rescue me.

Please, someone, rescue me.

Eventually, the panic would wake me, and I'd bolt upright, sweating and heaving as I tried to orient myself to my surroundings, relieved it wasn't real.

But the thing about recurring nightmares... they have some origin in reality, which was why it always felt so authentic.

And the nightmare I was currently having was the most realistic one yet.

Pinching myself for the third time, I *prayed* this was a vivid nightmare, not my actual life. It had to be some cosmic joke because there was no way this was real.

Brandon wouldn't do this to me. He just couldn't.

Blinking as I tried to keep myself upright, my head swiveled around the dancing bodies, looking for a clue to my rescue. Nothing but smiling faces greeted me as they step-ball-changed in synchronization with the beat. The music finally trailed off as their choreography ended, and they blended into the crowd, melting into the growing onlookers like what had just happened didn't.

The growing crowd outside the baseball stadium peered at me—that ever-present sense of waiting pressing into me—with twinkles in their eyes as the scene unfolded, their phones recording it for everyone to see.

Okay, nightmare, I see you've upped the imagery this

time—nothing like a full-blown threat of embarrassment to really freak me out. I can wake up now.

Sweat trailed down my back, my shirt sticking to me as the humidity grew around me, pressing in and invading my lungs. It might be autumn, but that didn't seem to matter in Florida. My breathing grew more rapid as reality clashed with my nightmare, and I pinched myself one last time.

The sharp sting of pain, the sweltering sun, and the buzz of conversation around me pushed me to accept the truth. There was no waking up from this nightmare.

This was so fucking real.

And now, not only would I have a massive bruise on my skin from the self-torture, but I had to face the fact that my boyfriend had just proposed to me in a crowd full of people with a flash mob.

A freaking flash mob!

The few dancers who lingered had ended their pose around Brandon, their arms stretched out as they high-lighted him with their jazz hands, and I wondered for the first time in five years if I even knew him. If he even knew *me*.

Because of all the ways I'd ever imagined a proposal, this wasn't even on the list. In fact, it was so far off the list it would take all the trees in the world to make enough paper to reach it.

Glancing at the smiling faces around me, I became overwhelmed as they urged me to respond to my boyfriend.

Okay, that so wasn't the urge I wanted.

This would be a great time to develop some super-powers. Warp manipulation, teleportation, flying... I really wasn't picky.

With no rescue in sight, I finally dropped my eyes and stared at my boyfriend.

Brandon Cupley was before me on bended knee, his light brown hair lying perfectly flat against his head. I never knew how he did that, considering he didn't spend much time on hair maintenance. But it was always flawless. His white button-down shirt was crisp, starched to within an inch of its life, and his black suit pants held no wrinkles, almost like they were afraid of disappointing him. He had a strong jaw, an average nose, and eyes the color of melted caramel.

And on occasion, when he smiled at something he really liked, a dimple would pop out of his right cheek, just as it was now. I gulped as I stared at it. Stupid dimple!

I'd never felt so betrayed by a dimple before.

I couldn't deny that Brandon was classically hand-some, had an excellent job at his father's accounting firm, and was always kind to his mother. In fact, he'd been the perfect boyfriend for the past five years. He was a good guy. The type parents loved and helped old ladies cross the street. He didn't excessively drink or smoke, and he never hit me. He followed all the rules and was as straight-laced as they came. There was no doubt we'd have a stable future together.

So what was halting me? Was stable good enough?

The longer I stood frozen without saying anything,

the more the dimple disappeared, and I picked at my nails, a clear sign my anxiety had ramped up even higher by attacking them.

This was it. I couldn't pass out and hope everyone forgot. A panic attack wouldn't save me this time. I had to give him an answer.

Glancing down at the object I'd been ignoring until now, I stared at the opened ring box. Brandon's shoulders relaxed as my eyes fell on the glittery diamond, his smile returning tenfold. He held it out to me like he was offering me the most precious gift in the entire world.

Sorry, dude. But my brother gave me that when he saved my life. Bone marrow trumped any diamond ring. Them's the facts.

"So, will you? Will you marry me, BB?"

You'd think I'd be jumping for joy, right? That I'd be ecstatic my boyfriend had just proposed to me in such a grand way. You'd probably even think I'd been dreaming and hoping about this for months.

Hate to break it to you, sis, but you'd be wrong.

Dread, fear, and an overwhelming sense of doom sat in my gut as I stared down at him, sheer panic in my eyes. I licked my lips as I tried to wet them, my mouth drying quicker than a desert as the suffocating pressure surrounded me. I didn't do big crowds, public speaking, or any type of activity where I was the central focus for this very reason.

Scanning the crowd, I finally recognized some faces; my mom smiled back at me with tears in her eyes, my dad and his—much younger—new girlfriend looked on with excitement, and my brother watched me with his protective stare in place, ready to jump in and save me as he always did.

How sad was it that I really wanted him to? I was twenty-four years old, and I needed my big brother to save me. I didn't know which was more pathetic—that fact or this proposal.

I always assumed I'd feel happy at this moment, but the only thing I felt was disappointment. A crushing, breath-stealing—make you wish a black hole would appear—disappointment.

Brandon didn't know me at all.

How could he, if he chose to propose this way? My literal nightmare.

And if he did presume to know me and still proposed this way, then that was even worse. He knew how I'd feel about this and decided to do it anyway. He hadn't taken my feelings into consideration and instead was selfish, liking how this would make him look in the eyes of everyone else.

We weren't alike at all, not how I thought, anyway.

My emotions warred inside of me as he gazed at me with confidence; no doubt in his mind that I'd say yes. I was, after all, the girl who never caused any waves, who felt privileged just to be alive, and who never wanted to be a burden. The reality was, I felt obligated to say yes… like I didn't have a choice.

And that made me feel dirty.

"I, uh, I…" My cheeks heated, and I twisted my hands more as the pit in my stomach opened wider.

This wasn't right. Nothing about this was right. Apprehension coated me like a fake fur coat, suffocating me in the heat to the point I felt lightheaded. Unfortunately, I had no way of knowing if it was the proposal itself or the fact it was Brandon doing it.

Geesh, that was a hard thing to think about my potential fiancé, but I didn't know how else to frame it. Being the center of attention as everyone stared at me *was* my literal worst fear, and this proposal was the fucking Olympics of my recurring nightmare.

Which brought me back around to hoping it was a nightmare because the man I loved and married should know that about me. And it wasn't like it was a big secret. In fact, it was common knowledge. I *loathed* being put on the spot. Always had. It was probably from all the unwanted attention my illness had brought me and growing up in the limelight, but now wasn't the time to dive deep into my psyche.

"Say yes! Say yes! Say yes!" the crowd chanted as they grew impatient. The volume rose, amping up my heart rate, and I knew I needed to get out of this situation immediately before I did something embarrassing like faint or pee my pants.

So I did the only thing I could do at that moment and prayed it was the right one.

"Um, yes." I grimaced, squeezing my eyes as I waited for the onslaught of embarrassment to hit me.

Brandon beamed at me, clearly not caring I looked more like I'd been asked to take a dump in the middle of the crowd and not to marry him. His dimple glinted as he stood and lifted me off my feet. His arms wrapped around me, and his classic mint scent engulfed me as he pressed my nose into his perfect ensemble. But it was better than seeing all the stares, so I wrapped my arms around him and held on for dear life.

My heart slowed, and my breathing returned to normal as he let me go, sliding the shiny diamond onto my finger.

"Did you love the proposal? I wanted to do something big to show you how much I love you. Bryce wasn't sure you'd go for it, but I knew you would. I just knew," Brandon gushed as both of our parents surrounded us.

It didn't surprise me that my brother had tried to stop this, and his earlier cagey behavior now made more sense; he was my best friend and the person who knew me the best. Sadness crept in when I realized it wasn't the man I was marrying.

"You're getting married!" my mother shouted, pulling me into her arms as she sobbed. "I never thought I'd see this day."

And there it was. The reminder that I'd been sick. That I'd almost died. That I shouldn't be alive today.

The fear. The worry. The burden I'd been.

Smiling, I nodded at my mother as I soothed her tears and fell into the role we were all comfortable with. The one where I smiled, so grateful to be healthy and alive, and reminded others just how fortunate we all were.

My entire purpose in life had been whittled down to

making others feel good about their choices. To be a reflection of the hard things they'd overcome and justify the perfect life they felt entitled to live now because of it.

I wasn't a person, but a prop.

"We'll need to go shopping immediately. I'm assuming you'll be planning for an early spring wedding. It will need to be before spring training, of course, and then there's your birthday," my mom prattled on as she talked to herself, already creating lists in her head.

"Wow, that quick?" I asked, my voice trembling.

"It's a big year for the team, BB. We won't want to miss any of it," my dad interjected.

Right. *The team.* The Columbus Blue Devils.

Dad had been a star baseball player for the Blue Devils most of my childhood, then retired and became the general manager of the Wilmington Yellowjackets, a AAA Minor league team in my preteens. By the time I was a teenager, he'd transitioned from team manager to team owner, buying his own baseball club—the Blue Devils *and* the Yellowjackets.

Bryce had followed in his footsteps and was drafted out of college. He'd moved through the farm system quickly and played in the Majors for the Blue Devils until the end of last season when he'd been injured, and sent to the Yellowjackets to recover. He was hoping to be back with the Blue Devils at the beginning of next season, but hadn't heard anything definite yet.

It didn't surprise me either that my mom still

accommodated baseball season despite having been divorced from my father for almost ten years now. The Bakers lived, breathed, and revolved around baseball. It was just how it was.

Brandon was the only person in my life who was separate from the Blue Devils. I looked up at him, and he smiled softly and reassuringly. He knew the love/hate relationship I had with the game.

And it wasn't that I hated it. Most of my best memories revolved around baseball. It was just that everything else came second.

Even the wedding I didn't want to have, apparently. But what else could I do? If I wanted my family there, then I had no other choice.

"Of course, Dad. Before spring training, it is." I smiled, but it was weak, and everyone resumed their planning as we headed into the stadium to watch the final game in the World Series—even our family vacations revolved around baseball. The Blue Devils hadn't made it to the postseason, but it didn't stop Dad and Bryce from wanting to attend the biggest game of the year.

Thank God Brandon hadn't proposed during the game. I most certainly would've died.

Small mercies, I supposed, but all I really wanted was to go back in time before this day even started. But since I also didn't have that superpower, I'd have to find some way to be happy about my upcoming nuptials.

Blake

TWO

MY FATHER BELIEVED that baseball could solve anything. Growing up, that meant anytime I had a problem, he would take me out to toss the ball back and forth until we had a solution. If it was a really serious one, we'd head to the batting cages and hit the ball until my arms hurt. I wasn't particularly good at any of it, my clumsiness and fatigue hindering any actual skills, but I enjoyed the time I spent with my dad. And if it was really bad, we'd go to a game—Little League, College, Minors, or Majors. It didn't matter as long as baseball was being played.

Like most little girls, I idolized my father. Steven Baker was larger than life. He played professional baseball, making his office the coolest. My brother, Bryce, and I spent as much time as we could at the ballpark. Everyone who worked at the stadium became our extended family, filling us with popcorn and bubblegum while my dad practiced. It was seriously the best.

And for the longest time, I believed my father. Baseball was the answer to everything.

That was until I'd gotten so sick that the treatments no longer worked, and the only thing that could save me was a bone marrow transplant. That day changed everything as my parents wrestled with what to do. How could fate be so cruel to make my brother the only match? Ensuring they'd have to choose between us.

It was the first time I saw my father cry, and I wished with everything I could that baseball would save me. Thankfully, Bryce and I had both come out of the surgeries well, but it put a dent in our previously pristine life.

It was the first time baseball had let me down. The second was my parents' divorce when I was fifteen, and the third… today.

True to my mother's word, she'd planned and executed the perfect wedding in four months. Today was February 11—my wedding day—three days before my twenty-fifth birthday and four days before spring training for the Blue Devils.

"Couldn't even help a girl out and be booked, could you?" I mumbled as I glared at the Blue Devil emblem hanging over the door. Because, of course, my wedding was taking place at Emerald Park, home of the Columbus Blue Devils.

I stared at my reflection in the mirror, my dress pure white and satin with just a hint of lace at the top. It was beautiful, but I felt like a fraud. I'd kept hoping that I'd finally have that "this is right" moment the closer the wedding date neared. But there wasn't an ounce of happiness inside me… only a foreboding feeling of terror.

Outwardly, my blonde hair was styled perfectly; every little strand I never seemed able to tame was pulled back in a flawless side braid. My blue eyes stood out more than ever, the black mascara and fake eyelashes making my eyes pop. Makeup artistry I could never recreate highlighted and bronzed my face into something you'd see on a magazine cover. My average looks had been transformed into a stunning woman, to the point I didn't recognize myself.

But for all intents and purposes, I looked like a beautiful bride ready to marry the man of her dreams.

I was the epitome of a classic and elegant bride, even if my shoes were cleats instead of heels and my bouquet was in the shape of a baseball. But with my veil perched just so on my head, you didn't even notice the oddness. The ring on my finger sparkled, mocking me as I tried to figure out what was wrong with my reflection.

Why wasn't I blushing? Or even smiling?

Clutching my stomach, I took a deep breath.

"I don't think baseball can solve this one, Dad," I whispered, the sound of my plea disrupting the quiet space. "There's no relief pitcher, and it's the bottom of the ninth with two outs." My lip wobbled at the thought.

No, there had to be something. I just needed to find the winning hit. The magic play that would bring the runners home. As Yogi Berra said, "It ain't over till it's over."

Pacing, I ignored how the cleats pinched as I tried to reassure myself this was what I wanted.

"You love Brandon. He's been there for you through school and your illness. He's solid." I paced some more, my breathing increasing as I tried to find more reasons to marry him. "He has that dimple you love!" I snapped my fingers, feeling victorious at remembering. "And… and…"

Shit. Had I really agreed to marry a man because he was consistent and had a dimple? Damn. I knew I didn't like to rock the boat, but when had I completely given up driving it?

Staring at myself in the mirror again, I knew the real reason I'd said yes to his proposal. It was the same reason I'd gotten my MBA despite having no intention of using it. The same reason I'd gone to college in my hometown, regardless of offers from universities across the United States. And the same reason, at twenty-five, I was still a virgin.

I'd spent my whole life playing it safe, doing what everyone else wanted.

It was hard not to when you'd spent the formative years of your life mainly living in hospitals being poked and prodded. Being born with a genetic disorder that wanted to kill you taught you to take each moment for what it was worth.

But somewhere along the way, I'd gotten scared and tired of seeing the fear on my parent's faces each time a new bruise would appear. So, instead of living, I existed.

Tears fell down my face, ruining the flawless makeup airbrushed hours ago.

What was the point of living if I let everyone else do it for me? When would it be enough? My penance for being born sick? For causing them to worry? For needing so much care?

When could I step away from the manacles of gratitude for saving my life?

Surely, when given a second chance, one wasn't expected to live from the shadows? To allow everyone else to feel better while you slowly drowned on the inside?

"I can't do this anymore."

My chin wobbled, and I could feel the sob crawling up my throat, ready to wrench itself free as all the pain and sadness from a life spent hiding, surfaced.

A knock at my door had me whipping around in a flurry of satin and tulle as I desperately searched for a place to hide, to run, to do anything but walk through that door and marry someone only because they'd asked me to in a crowd and I'd been too chicken to say no. A cute dimple could do a lot, but a lifetime of commitment wasn't one of them.

"BB, you ready?" my brother asked as he opened the door, freezing when his brown eyes met mine. "Shit. Okay. Um. What do you need? Who should I kill?" he asked rapidly as he hurried into the room, closing the door behind him.

And this was why I loved my brother. Not only had he saved my life as a young boy by giving me his bone marrow, but he was truly my best friend, protector, and biggest ally.

His warm hands landed on my arms, running up and down them as he transferred his heat into me. He didn't rush me but gave me the time to find the words.

"I've been such a fool. A scared idiot. I've been standing here, staring at my reflection and realizing that I hated everything about how I looked and had no idea why I was marrying Brandon."

"I don't know, Blanket. The raccoon look you got going on is pretty you."

A choked sob and half laugh bubbled out at the childhood nickname as my tears and snot splattered down my face. Bryce lifted his brow, daring me to prove him wrong.

"Not that you didn't look gorgeous, but I had wondered why you went along with all of Mom's choices." He grimaced as he scanned me.

"It was just easier to let her have her way. She was so happy and kept saying how she thought at one time she'd never get to experience this moment with me. How could I tell her, Bry? She's been miserable since the divorce, and I—"

"It's not your fault, Sis. You have to stop blaming yourself for everything that went wrong." He narrowed his eyes, daring me to protest.

I let out a shaky breath, finally hearing the message he'd been saying all these years. *It wasn't my fault.*

"Now, what do you need? I'm assuming you're not going to marry the nightstand?"

"Nightstand?" I asked, quirking my brow as I tried to figure out the reference.

"Yeah. Sorry, but he's about as bright and useful as one."

My jaw fell open as I gaped at my brother. He stood proud, with his arms crossed, not ashamed of his comment. That was the thing about Bryce; he never apologized for who he was.

"No, I can't marry Brandon," I said once I'd recovered, shaking my head for emphasis.

"Good. I wasn't looking forward to spending the holidays with him. I get that not everyone loves baseball, but the dude thinks a grand slam is what you order at Denny's. Add in the fact that Dad would've snapped if he brought up cricket one more time."

Grimacing, I suddenly wondered how anyone in my family had thought it was a good idea for me to marry Brandon. Had we all become too scared to say anything?

"How do I get out of here? I can't walk down that aisle. With everyone looking at me, I won't be able to say no. It would be too much pressure. Not to mention I don't want to embarrass him. Despite being dull, he's been a good friend to me. He's not a bad guy."

Bryce groaned but nodded. "We have different definitions of friends, but fine." He rubbed his hands together, a mischievous smile spreading across his face. "Time for Operation Cleat Retreat. Leave the distraction up to me. I feel like I've been preparing for this my whole life."

I huffed, crossing my arms as I tried to hide my nervousness. "You seriously need to get out more. You're becoming like Dad with how much time you spend at the sports complex. Plus, I'm not sure this situation is how that phrase works. Didn't Hawk coin it to run out on cleat chasers?"

Bryce ignored me and rolled his eyes as he pulled out his phone and hit a button. "Hey, I need you to pull your car around to the side entrance and take BB somewhere no one will look for the night."

"Why does that sound like you're sending me off with an ax murderer?" I mumbled, debating if this was really the lesser of two evils.

Bryce narrowed his eyes at me but said nothing. "Yeah, leave now. Just say there's a flower emergency or some shit. I'll head off the others while you escape. Yeah, thanks, man."

He disconnected the call and shoved his phone back into his suit pants. "Hawk's on his way. Stay with him until morning. Give it time to blow over."

At the mention of his best friend, butterflies I hadn't felt all day erupted in my belly as my heart picked up speed. I licked my lips, and my cheeks blushed as heat and desire rolled through me. Crap, crap, crap.

I hurried around the room, throwing what I could see into a bag to keep myself from looking at Bryce. It had been years since I'd sworn that my childhood crush on his best friend had disappeared. I didn't want him to see how big of a lie that was when Hawk was the key to my escape.

Kicking off the torturous shoes, I slipped on my hot pink high tops and grabbed my purse as I yanked the veil off my head. Bryce peeked out the door, telling someone I'd be just a minute before he shut it and motioned for me to go out the other.

Thank you, Emerald Stadium, for having a million escape routes!

"Go, go." He waved me off, one last look of concern on his face as

I ducked out the door with my bag clutched to my chest. My heart raced now that I'd finally decided to do something for myself.

"Wait!" Bryce called, stopping me in my tracks. He ran up to me and pulled me into a hug. I instantly wrapped my arms around him, loving how safe and cared for I always felt in my brother's arms. "I'm proud of you, BB. Love you more than tacos." He kissed my cheek before he turned me and pushed me out of the door just as someone rounded the corner. I could hear him talking, but I didn't focus on it and took off down the stairs. My steps echoed around me, my breathing loud as I prayed not to run into anyone.

Pushing through the exit door, I looked both ways before I spotted Hawk's Mustang idling at the curb. Pumping my legs, the white dress flew around me as I ran through the frozen grass. The door opened as I neared, and I slid into the front seat, the feeling of home registering around me as fresh-cut grass and sandal-wood engulfed me.

Gazing into Hawk's mismatched eyes, our gazes locked, and we held each other's stare. My heart flipped over as it felt like we stole a second just for ourselves.

Maybe baseball hadn't failed me this time after all, and I'd just been given the curve ball I needed.

HAWK

THREE

I HATED WEDDINGS. They felt too orchestrated for my taste. I didn't like people telling me how I should feel about something in general, but weddings took the cake. Every detail was planned to showcase the couple's love, attempting to convince you that these two people were about to make the most beautiful commitment to one another.

In my experience, monogrammed napkins and color schemes had nothing to do with love. In fact, it seemed like the more effort and detail that went into the decor, the less likely the couple would make it to five years.

Not that I was a relationship expert or anything. I steered clear of any romantic entanglements and focused solely on my career. People depended on me to support them, and I wouldn't let my little sister down, even if she didn't think she needed it anymore.

She did. They all did.

Despite my belief and abhorrence of weddings, I'd

donned my suit and stood dutifully at the makeshift aisle as I waited for this charade to begin.

Shuffling on my feet, I glanced around the room and took in all the smiling faces. Having played Little League with Bryce, I'd known the Bakers since I was eight years old. He took one look at my scowling face and decided right then we were going to be best friends. Considering I'd never had a friend before, much less one as shiny as him, I couldn't help but be intrigued by his proclamation. Like it was that easy to decide to be friends with me.

Everything else in my life disagreed with him, so I couldn't help but wonder how it would play out. Twenty years later, I stood sentry at his little sister's wedding and ignored the weird feeling in my gut.

"You think your team has what it takes to make a play for the big show this year?" one of Bryce's uncles asked.

I cleared my throat and dropped my eyes down to the man. I didn't like speculating, but I couldn't dismiss these people like I did the media or strangers.

"That's the hope," I grumbled, spreading my feet and crossing my arms. This was the third conversation of this type I'd been pulled into in the past hour.

For some reason, it was intriguing that Bryce and I played for opposing teams. But in the Majors, you didn't get to pick your team, and I'd been drafted by the Kansas City Tornados six years ago while the Columbus Blue Devils had drafted Bryce. We didn't get to see each other as much now, but the distance hadn't changed our friendship.

We were solid. Bryce was a part of me, and not even baseball rivalries could change that.

The man grunted, surveying the crowd before he geared up for his next question. Thankfully, my phone vibrated in my pocket, and I lifted a finger to stop him from speaking. The man frowned but stayed quiet.

Ah, bliss. Small talk had to be the armpit of the wedding facade.

Withdrawing my phone, I stepped away when Bryce's name appeared. He spoke before I even said hello.

"Hey, I need you to pull your car around to the side entrance and take Blake somewhere no one will look for the night."

"Right now?" I asked, peering around as I looked for my escape route. I didn't need to know the why. Our friendship was built on complete trust. If he needed me, I was there. No questions asked. There were no secrets between us.

Outside of baseball and my family, Bryce's friendship was the most coveted thing in my life. Without sounding too sappy, knowing him had changed my life.

"Yeah, leave now. Just say there's a flower emergency or some shit. I'll head off the others while you escape."

"Flowers. Right. Okay. I'm on my way," I said as I ducked around a few people.

"Yeah, thanks, man."

I couldn't decide if something terrible had occurred since Bryce sounded far too chipper for anything I kept imagining if it was my little sister who was getting married.

"Hawk! Have you seen Bryce?" Candice Baker asked, stopping me before I could make my getaway.

"Oh, um, he said something about flowers. I'm going to help him now."

"Flowers?" Bryce's mom scrunched up her nose in thought, contrasting with the rest of her. Her blonde hair was swept up in an updo; her silver dress was classy and sophisticated for her daughter's wedding. "Hmm, well, thank you for helping him. Tell him to hurry. The ceremony is about to start." She patted my arm as she turned to track down her next victim.

I sighed in relief and knew it was only her preoccupation with the wedding that allowed me to escape.

Candice Baker, or Candi as she preferred to go by, was a force to be reckoned with. She wasn't just a pretty face but a cutthroat sports lawyer. Candi hadn't been the typical soft and cuddly mom. She was used to getting her way and being in control, and the only time I'd ever seen her fall apart had been when Blake's diagnosis came to light. It wasn't something she could negotiate or control, which left her uncharacteristically vulnerable.

Those years were hard for everyone, but I think it affected Candi the most. I felt marginally bad about lying to the woman who was a surrogate mother to me, especially if it was about to ruin her happiness. From her standpoint, Blake getting married was the pot of gold at the end of the rainbow. It was how she measured happiness for all those painful years.

I disagreed, but I had my own issues with marriage that clouded my opinion.

Pushing through the door, I trotted down the stairs and into the cold air. I didn't miss the Ohio weather and looked forward to returning to Kansas City in a few days. My black Mustang with red racing stripes came into view as I entered the back parking lot. Candi had negotiated a great deal for me when I signed my first contract, and I'd been given a large signing bonus. My car was the one thing I'd bought for myself. In every other area of my life, I remained frugal, too aware of how quickly this lifestyle could disappear, and I had people depending on me.

My Mustang was my measure of success, a reminder that my hard work had paid off. Each time I slid into it, I felt the same happiness I had the first time I settled into the leather seats. It was something no one could ever take away from me. That was a powerful thing.

The engine's rumble vibrated beneath me as exhilaration raced up my spine. Shifting it into reverse, I drove to the side exit of Emerald Stadium that Bryce mentioned.

Just as I pulled up, the side exit flew open, and a vision in a white dress raced to my car. The white material spread behind her like a cape, a superhero angel making her escape. I tried to gauge if something had happened, but I couldn't see shit from here. Leaning over, I pushed open the door just before she crashed into the seat.

The air heated around us as I stared into blue eyes I knew as well as my own. Surveying Blake's face, I took in the black mascara streaks and her puffy eyes. Her hair was still meticulously pulled back into a braid, falling over her shoulder, the end resting on her chest. I watched as it rose with each breath she took until I remembered it was my best friend's little sister I was perving on.

Locking eyes with her, I searched for something to say. She looked… *different*.

And I didn't think it was just the hundreds of dollars of makeup on her face. Blake's eyes swirled with emotion, and I tried to decipher what they were.

Hope? Fear? Gratitude?

No, that didn't feel right. It was more charged than that… more *innocent*. Almost like she saw me as a white knight swooping in to rescue her on horseback.

This might be a Mustang, but I was no white knight.

Nothing good would come from her looking at me like that.

It didn't matter that the sick feeling I had in my gut all day had disappeared, or how hard my heart thumped in my chest at her nearness.

Or how much I liked her looking at me the way she did.

This wasn't who I was in her story. I couldn't be.

Clearing my throat, I turned back to the front and

tightened my hands on the wheel before stealing another glance.

"You good?" I asked, ignoring how raw my voice sounded.

"Yeah. I am now. Thanks, Hawk."

"No problem, Blazy. You know how it is. If Bry says jump, I don't even ask how high." I said the words, but they tasted bitter in my mouth, their meaning like sawdust on my tongue. Our relationship was more than that, and it didn't feel fair to the three of us for me to classify it that way, but I couldn't take them back now.

Shifting the car, I turned the knob for the radio, needing something to drown out the silence that had become oppressive.

As I headed onto the highway, I tried to think of a place to take Blake. I had to assume she was running away from her wedding and people would be looking for her, wanting answers.

Tapping my fingers on the steering wheel, I debated my options. I didn't live in town anymore, and there was no way I'd take her to my old house. My sister had her second child a few months ago, so it would be chaotic there. Not to mention that Wren was horrible at keeping secrets. She'd spill to the first person who asked her.

"I can't believe I just did that," Blake whispered, her breathing increasing. I glanced over, taking in her hands as she twisted them in the fabric, her nails mere stubs. She looked up, her eyes watering and horrified as she stared at me.

Shit. I didn't do tears.

Taking the next exit, I swerved into the first lot I saw and parked the car. Facing her, my hands wavered in front of me as I tried to figure out how to make the tears stop. Did I wave them around? Was there a call sign for this? Panic inched up my throat as her tears fell harder.

"He was a bit of a tool, if you ask me," I blurted, catching her off guard. "Anyone who hates pizza can't be trusted. Plus, he didn't understand baseball at all."

"I kind of liked that," she admitted, sniffling her nose, the tears slowing.

"Yeah, well. It might've been cute for a while, but imagine it five years down the road. There's no way your father or brother wouldn't come to blows with him."

"Maybe." She shrugged one shoulder, her eyes fixed on her hands. How did a shoulder appear so sad? I needed to keep talking. She stopped crying when I spoke.

"What made you want to marry him in the first place?" I asked, curious and hoping I hadn't just poked the wound.

"The proposal," she started. I snorted, shaking my head, and cut her off. I couldn't believe it.

"Seriously? I didn't take you for a girl to like something like that. It sounded idiotic to me. Like he wanted to prove to everyone how romantic and thoughtful he was. If you're going to make that commitment to someone, it should be private. No one else needs to be involved in that. That way, once she says yes, you can celebrate by fucking on any available surface."

"Eep! Um." Blaze coughed, fanning her face. "Actually, I was going to say I only said yes because I just wanted the proposal over. I hated every second of it." Her face turned tomato red, and she kept waving her hands, her voice growing higher and faster as she spoke. "What you said sounds nice. More my speed. Except for the whole sex thing. I wouldn't know."

"What the fuck?" I scoffed, glaring at her like she was spinning the worst bullshit ever. "No way you're a virgin."

She rolled her eyes; some of the fearless Blake I knew as a kid emerged as she stopped her hand dance.

"Hate to break it to you, Hawkster, but it's true. Brandon wanted to wait until we were married. So unless you plan to test for yourself, you're gonna have to take my word for it."

I swallowed at her words, trying to hide the heat that hit me at her taunt. Fucking hell. I could not have these types of thoughts about her.

"Well, damn." I ignored how raspy my voice was.

"Yeah. Damn," she agreed, leaning back in the seat and crossing her arms as she stared out the windshield. It was back to being quiet in the car, but the tears had completely stopped.

"When it came down to it, I just couldn't imagine being married to him. He's nice and all, but I dunno; maybe it's naïve, but I wanted more. I've played it safe most of my life and tried to make it easier for everyone else." She turned to me, her blue eyes holding mine hostage again. "I'm tired of living for everyone else."

She licked her lips, and my eyes dropped on their own accord. My heart raced, and my face flushed as need rushed through me. No matter how much my brain said this wasn't right, my body disagreed.

"Where are we going to go? I'd really like to get out of this dress."

Do not think of her naked. Do not think of her naked.

I didn't think she was saying these things to torture me; her naïveté making more sense now. But it didn't mean my body wasn't responding to everything all the same. My cock thickened against my leg, pressing into my zipper, and I shifted, hoping she didn't notice.

"I have an idea," I mumbled, realizing that the last place anyone would look would be the most obvious. Turning back onto the road, I pulled into the parking lot of the hotel all the guests were staying at a few minutes later.

"Here?" she asked, giving me a skeptical look.

"Yep." I nodded, not saying anything else. Reaching into the back, I grabbed my favorite hoodie and gave it to her. "Put this on, and I'll let you in the side door."

Blake did as I asked and collected her bag as she exited my car. She pulled the hood up, letting the hoodie fall over her dress to cover most of her body. I held in the groan at how sexy I suddenly found that.

I nodded to the door and sprinted toward the front with my bag bouncing against my back. Tonight would be the most challenging test of friendship I'd ever faced.

Blake

FOUR

HUDDLED IN HAWK'S SWEATSHIRT, I attempted to ignore how amazing it smelled as I shuffled from one foot to the next. I couldn't believe I'd blurted out I was a virgin. What was I expecting? Him to offer himself up as tribute?

Um, yeah. You totally did.

Shaking my head at myself, I replayed the conversation back in my head, mortified at everything I said. It was no wonder he only saw me as Bryce's little sister.

Now that the impending doom of getting married to someone I didn't love was gone, I could feel the weight as it lifted off my shoulders, and a sense of peace filled me.

No matter what happened from here, I'd done the right thing. I wish I'd been braver sooner, so I wouldn't have caused as many aftershocks, though.

My parents. Brandon. Brandon's parents.

They'd all want an explanation, and I didn't have it

in me at the moment to explain. If I could get through the night without anyone cornering me, I'd be ready to face the masses tomorrow. Maybe.

The wind whipped around me, chilling me further as I curled into myself more. Shoving my hands into the front pocket, I grimaced when my fingers brushed against something sharp. My hand wrapped around the object, carefully pulling it out without further injury. Unfurling my fingers, I blinked as I stared at the object, convinced I was hallucinating.

How was it even possibly here?

One way I'd coped as a sick kid was by collecting little pins that I'd covered my bookbag in. Some were motivational sayings, whereas others were objects I just liked. Since everyone had called me Bee or BB most of my life, I had an obsession with bees and, therefore, a lot of bee pun pins.

One had a little bee with "Beeoch" on it, which my mother found offensive, thus making it my favorite. At some point in my teens, I'd lost it. I'd searched my entire room from top to bottom for weeks but never could find it.

And somehow, it had ended up in Hawk's hoodie. Had it been here the whole time, or had he found it?

Before I could ponder the reasoning, the door flew open, and I shoved my hands back into the pocket, keeping them wrapped around the pin. Hawk lifted a brow at me when I didn't immediately step into the hotel.

Right. Runaway bride here.

The absurdity of the thought had me laughing out loud, the sound jerking Hawk's head toward me.

"Sorry. It's just... yeah." I gestured down to the hoodie/white dress combo I had going on. "I'm in a wedding gown."

Hawk stopped his stroll and stared at me. He'd been doing that a lot since I'd gotten into his car, and I couldn't figure out what it meant. Did I look funny? I probably resembled a little girl playing dress-up to him, not to mention the raccoon look Bryce said my face resembled.

My stomach rumbled loudly, breaking up the moment. Covering my mouth, I chuckled as I glanced down.

"Any chance we can get some food?" I asked, glancing back up at him. Hawk rubbed his chin, a peppering of facial hair on his youthful face.

"I have an idea, but we gotta be stealthy."

Hawk reached out and grabbed my hand, pulling me along down the hallway. I knew he'd said something, but the instant his hand made contact, all thoughts ceased to exist.

Hawk's large palm wrapped around mine, the roughness speaking to all the nights he spent catching. I followed in a haze as he hurried down the hotel's first floor. The blue carpet with gold dots swirled around me, and I vaguely caught sight of the plain walls with generic paintings.

My heart thumped loudly, and I worried he'd hear it any second now. Not that I could say anything. All my words had become caught in my throat, which felt full of cotton. Was I losing my mind? Having an episode? Surely this wasn't how people always felt when touching a hot guy?

There was no doubt Hawk was attractive. He had the whole bad boy look down pat with his faux hawk and shaved sides, the tips dyed to match his team colors during the season. Today it was his regular brown and brushed down, the long pieces falling into his mismatched eyes each time he turned his head. He had a slight gash through one eyebrow and a small scar on his chin from a fall off his bicycle.

I knew his face almost as well as my brother's, considering it was rare for them to ever be apart. But rarely did I get the chance to stare so openly at him. Whenever he caught me staring as a kid, he'd stick out his tongue or make a funny face to make me laugh. He'd been good at that when I could barely get off the couch.

As I grew older, my cheeks would heat, and I'd turn away, embarrassed for getting caught gawking. Then, at some point, I pushed Hawk out of my mind, content to focus on Brandon. During that time, he'd gotten a few tattoos and piercings, though none were visible today since he wore a suit.

And boy, did he wear it well.

His catcher's bubble butt filled the back, his thick thighs stretching against the material with each step. His broad chest had the white dress shirt straining with each twist of his muscles. I honestly didn't know which version I preferred to drool over—in his catcher gear or this suit.

"Follow my lead."

"Hmm," I said, realizing he'd said something. I'd been staring at his butt, and as he glanced back to check on me, I wondered if he'd caught me. My cheeks flushed hotter at the thought, and I stared, waiting for him to tell me what he'd said.

"Keep the hood up and let me do the talking."

I saluted him, and he snickered, shaking his head at my gesture. Hawk peeked into a door and pulled me in after him. The sound of pans clanging and water spraying hit my ears as we crept down a hall. We stopped with our backs against a wall outside a door, and Hawk lifted his finger to his lips. I nodded in understanding as he went back to watching.

When I'd suggested food, I hadn't thought it would involve espionage, but with the way my heart raced and my energy spiked, I couldn't deny I was enjoying it. It was the most fun I'd had in a while, and it kept me from wondering what everyone back at Emerald Park was doing.

Hawk tugged on my hand, and we were moving again. I had to assume we were in some back tunnel of the hotel for staff. I could hear different things going on past the walls we passed. One room sounded like a Bar Mitzvah and another a high school reunion. Amazingly, we hadn't been spotted yet, and I hoped our luck would continue.

As my face planted into his back next, I realized he'd

stopped suddenly. I rubbed my nose as I tried to hear what they were saying.

"Owie. Your back's too hard."

"Shh, Blazy," he whispered, his eyes dropping to my face just as a conversation drifted to us.

"Who had today's wedding being canceled in the pot?"

"I think it was Craig," another voice responded. "What do they want us to do with the food?"

"Box it up. Take what you want, and the rest is to be donated to a food pantry."

"I'll let the others know."

"Perfect timing," Hawk whispered, glancing down at me.

Oh. It was *my* wedding reception. Bittersweet emotions rolled through me at the knowledge. Hawk linked our fingers and ducked to peer into a door before opening it.

"Grab stuff, but be quick," he said, nodding at the food.

I froze as I stared at the plates of food, not sure what I wanted. But Hawk's movement sent me into motion, and I grabbed a box and began to fill it, not paying much attention to what it was. I grabbed some napkins and shoved them into my pocket when my box was full. Passing some bread, I grabbed a few rolls and shoved them down the front of my dress before picking up a fork.

"Let's go," Hawk hissed, and I quickly snagged a few more things, not focusing on what they were, just wanting things. I made it to the door as someone else entered, and we both froze to the spot.

"Hey! You're not supposed to be back here," he said, recovering first. My face flamed at being caught as embarrassment overwhelmed me.

Nope. Not today! Anger and frustration at never standing up for myself poured out of me onto the unsuspecting hotel worker.

"It's my wedding!" I shouted. "I deserve to eat some of this food, at least!" I hit my chest, brandishing the fork still in my hand like a cutlery weapon.

The server stopped, his eyes widening at my outburst. His eyes ran over me, taking in my wedding dress beneath the hoodie. He raised his hands and nodded, some softness entering his features.

"Yeah. Sure. Whatever you want." He paused and picked up something, but I kept my focus on him. "Here, take this too."

He handed me a pink box, and I placed it on top of the one I held possessively to my chest and backed away like he might try to steal it. I spotted a bottle of champagne by the door and wrapped my fork-laden hand around it.

"I'm taking this too," I dared, waiting for him to chase after me or something.

"Of course." He nodded, keeping his hands lifted in surrender

"You never saw me."

"I never saw you," he agreed. He was no longer afraid but smiled and gave me a reassuring nod.

"Thank you!" I yelled before ducking out the door with a huge smile on my face.

Damn. That felt good.

Hawk was already out there, his eyes wide as he attempted to keep his laugh contained, his face turning red with the effort.

"That. Was. Badass. Blazy," he wheezed, clutching his ribs.

I lifted my head, accepted his praise, and walked away from the kitchen with my wedding feast bounty, like the ninja bride I was.

Hawk recovered and walked next to me, his arms as full as mine, and I couldn't help but grin at the image. The edges of his mouth lifted in an uncharacteristic smile as we walked side by side. I peeked at him out of the corner of my eyes, pleased with his praise.

I didn't want him to see me as a child or the crazy girl who ran away crying because her boyfriend hadn't wanted to have sex with her before marriage. I knew I shouldn't care what he thought, but I couldn't help it.

First crushes were hard to shake.

Voices grew louder down the hall, and I stopped, wondering if the next person would be as accommodating as the last server. Before I could contemplate what to do, Hawk's strong arm pulled me into a closet, our food containers pressed between us as we stared at one another in the dark space. I could feel his eyes on me, and I wished I knew what he was thinking.

But Hawk was a vault. Always had been. Rarely did he share with anyone what he felt. Most of the time, he was stoic and grumpy with his hardass catcher face on the field, which was just a more intense version of his regular face. The man did not smile. *Ever.*

It made me appreciate the one I'd elicited earlier even more.

He cleared his throat, the air around us growing hot as the tension built and our faces grew closer. Though, I was confident it was all in my head and only one-sided.

Because there was no way it looked like Hawk Anderson wanted to kiss me.

"I think it's clear," he grunted.

"Clear?" I asked, my brain not understanding. He nodded to the door, and I caught up, glad for the dark as my cheeks flamed.

Right. Not a kiss.

The rest of the journey was uneventful as we returned to the door leading to the lobby. From there, we made it to the elevator, and only a few people looked at me oddly as they spotted my dress. Thankfully, I didn't look completely out of place since Hawk was still in his suit. When an older woman smiled, I knew she thought we were a newly married couple.

"Congratulations," she said as we stepped onto our floor.

Hawk raised his eyebrow in question, not understanding her comment. Cheeks heated, I nodded to her and gave a small thanks as the doors closed.

Hawk kept peering at me, waiting for an explanation as we walked to his room. Sighing, I kept my eyes focused forward as we came to a door.

"She thought we were newlyweds," I answered as he pushed the keycard into the lock. He froze, his mouth dropping open slightly before he rallied and opened the door, pushing for me to enter first.

"Um, I suppose you want to get out of that dress. Do you have clothes?" he asked as we sat the food down. When I started to pull food and other things out of my pockets, he froze in amusement and watched me, smirking as I kept tugging things free.

"Anything else?" he asked, grinning at me as he watched.

"Oh, yes." I lifted my finger as I reached into my dress and pulled out the rolls. Hawk snorted, and I felt oddly satisfied with my efforts.

"Boob bread. My favorite."

My cheeks heated as my heart flipped, but it felt like a win in the "not a kid" column. He knew I had boobs. *Winner, winner, bread for dinner.*

"Clothes?" he asked again, and I pulled my bag around and glanced through it.

Glasses. Makeup wipes. Phone. Money. Charger. Underwear. Medication. Toothbrush.

"Nope. I didn't have a lot of time to plan. Bryce said go, so I grabbed what was in reach and ran."

Hawk grunted but went over to his suitcase, placing a duffle bag next to it. I took the time to assess the room, not surprised at how orderly it was. Hawk was a clean freak, and everything had its place and order. He unzipped the black case, and my mouth dropped open at the tidiness of his clothes.

"Even your suitcase is meticulous!"

"How else would it be? If you don't do it right, things get wrinkled."

"Wrinkles are the least of my worries."

He didn't say anything to that, handing me a pair of athletic shorts, boxer briefs, and a white undershirt.

"You can use the bathroom first."

Nodding, I took my bag into the bathroom, dropped the borrowed clothes, and took inventory. My hair wasn't as much of a mess as I expected. I guess the sheer amount of products she used held it together. My face had makeup tracks on it, so I used the cleaner and removed it and the fake lashes. Once that was done, I removed the awful contacts and put on my glasses.

"Already feel more human."

Pulling off the hoodie, I set it aside, determined not to give it back. Staring at myself in the mirror in my dress, I took in my silhouette. While the dress was lovely, it hadn't ever felt like *the* dress. I hadn't had a moment where I cried or gushed. It was just a pretty dress.

After a few minutes of attempting to unbutton all the million tiny ones on the back, I gave up and opened the door.

"Um, Hawk, I need some help."

He stepped into the bathroom with his eyes shielded.

"I'm dressed. I just can't get the buttons undone."

His hand dropped at my words, and he looked at me. I watched as he swallowed like he was talking himself into something. It also appeared like his cheeks were rosy, but it was hard to tell in this lighting and with his stubble.

Without a word, he moved behind me and unfastened the tiny pearls along the back with fingers more nimble than mine. Now and then, his fingers would graze against my bare skin, and I had to bite my cheek to stop myself from gasping.

"There," he muttered and bolted out the door, closing it behind him before I could even say thank you.

"Geez. I didn't think being in a room with a girl was that difficult," I muttered, sliding the dress off and letting it puddle around my feet. Putting on his shirt and shorts, I left the boxers on the counter since I didn't need them. Tying the strings tight to keep them from falling, I pulled the hoodie back on, smiling at the action.

Gathering my stuff, I left the bathroom and found him lounging on the bed.

The one and only bed.

Gulp.

He'd already changed out of his suit into a pair of gray sweatpants—help me, Jesus—and a tight black tank. The food was placed in the middle, with all the boxes opened and two makeshift plates in spots. He flipped through the channels but stopped, glancing at me as I entered.

Hawk's eyes trailed over my body, bringing goosebumps to my skin before he noticed the bundle I held. Hopping off the bed, he took the dress from me and placed it carefully over the back of a chair as I sat everything else on the dresser.

"Dig in." He nodded to the food, resuming his lounging position at the end.

Sitting on the other side, I picked up the stolen fork and looked at everything we'd gathered. There was steak, mashed potatoes, chicken, broccoli casserole, salad, macaroni and cheese, and even fried apples. It was a food coma waiting to happen. Taking a forkful of potatoes, I lifted it to him.

"Happy wedding feast."

"Happy wedding feast," he said, giving me another rare smile.

It was silent as we ate and watched an old movie on the TV, both of us in our own worlds as we gorged on the food.

"Oh, I got you something," he said, startling me. He grabbed a smaller box off the side table and held it out to me.

Lifting the lid, I didn't know if I should cry or laugh at what lay inside.

Blake

FIVE

I BLINKED at the wedding cake, shock and glee winning in the end, and a laugh bubbled out of me as I caught sight of the topper. I picked it up and held it out for Hawk to see. His mismatched eyes were soft as he stared at me, one corner of his mouth tilted up in an almost smile.

"Seriously? How did my mom think this was okay?"

The groom resembled a superhero, opening his shirt and showing the letter "B" on his chest, while the bride looked uncannily like Sandy from *Grease* before she went all black leather and curls. Her high ponytail mimicked my usual one, but the conservative dress and pink lips, as she stared adoringly at her groom, made my eyes roll. It was the most ridiculous thing I'd ever seen, highlighting just how insane marrying Brandon had been.

"Oh god." I covered my mouth, my eyes wide as

horror filtered through me. "I would've been B Cup. We'd be the B&B Cups," I wailed.

Hawk scrunched up his nose and tilted his head. "I thought his last name was Cupley?"

Narrowing my eyes, I threw the '50s housewife-like bride at him. "Same difference. Blake and Brandon Cupley." My body shuddered. "It's like I've been sleep-walking through life for the past ten years. Why on earth would I marry someone with the same initials? It's bad enough having Bryce with the same. People are always sending us the wrong things as it is. You don't even want to know how many cleat chaser's gifts I've been on the wrong end of." I gagged, remembering the last one.

My mind raced with this new revelation, my earlier numbness evaporating as the reality of the situation smacked me in the face. My life had been so hollow, so vacant. I might as well have been a doll because the only purpose I served was arm candy. Mediocre arm candy at best since I barely wore make-up and was most comfortable in ponytails and high tops.

"Clearly, I chose the easiest path and didn't question anything! What has my life become?" My tone grew more high-pitched as I spoke, panic and daunting horror overtaking me.

"You're more of a Frenchie than a Sandy," Hawk mumbled, fixated on the bride topper in his hand.

"Not the point!" I shrieked, finally catching his attention, and ignored how his comment made my heart leap. *Why did he know me better? I'm obviously more of the oddball sidekick than the main character.*

Hawk glanced up, his eyes bulging as he took in my panicked state, and he quickly sat up from his lounging position. He grabbed a fork and stuck it into the pie the attendant had given me. When the fork was full, he shoved it into my mouth, stopping my shrieks.

Sugary sweetness hit my tongue as fruit and meringue melted in my mouth. He withdrew the fork slowly like I was a scared animal about to attack. As the sugar settled into my system, I did calm a smidgeon. Damn him.

Hawk refilled the fork and lifted it again but stopped, this time to sniff it. Just as he did, I felt the tell-tale sign of cotton filling my mouth as my tongue started to numb.

"Shit! Where did you get that pie?" he asked, leaping off the bed and taking the fork and pie with him.

"The server gave it to me. Why?"

He didn't answer as he searched through my bag. I didn't even care, more focused on the weird feeling in my mouth.

"My tongue feels funny." I stuck it out and touched it, wondering why it felt bigger than usual and like it had a ball of yarn wrapped around it.

"Here." Hawk shoved a pink pill in my mouth and lifted a water bottle to my lips.

"You're being nice," I mumbled as I drank, trying not to spill the water.

"Don't freak out, Blazy, but…"

"But what?" I asked, craving more of that pie. I looked around, trying to find where he'd taken it.

"That pie wasn't from your reception. At least, I hope it wasn't, considering it had mango in it."

"Mango." I shook my head. "No, that's impossible. I'm allergic to mango."

Hawk lifted his brow as he continued to make me take sips of water. Oh. Right. The funny feeling on my tongue.

"Damn. Mango tastes good." I sighed as I finished the water and leaned back against the pillows. "Thanks," I said, realizing he'd just saved me from an embarrassing experience.

It was one thing to run out of your wedding; it was another to end up in the ER for an allergic reaction on the same night. My mother would never let me out of her sight if that happened.

My mother.

"Shit. I bet Mom is freaking out. This is the longest I've ever been without contact," I admitted, turning my head to stare at Hawk. He was lying back on the bed, his hands locked on his chest.

"Bryce will take care of Candi. Eat some cake. It will help counteract the meds."

Not having to be told twice, I grabbed a new fork and picked up the box. I slid the utensil into the icing and moaned around the tines as I licked it off.

"Okay. Mom got the cake right, at least."

Hawk cleared his throat, turning on his side and

shifting, his pupils dilated more than usual. "You didn't pick out your own wedding cake?"

"Nope. Mom picked out everything. I know she did it out of love, but yeah, it kind of sucks. Felt more like she was marrying Brandon than me." His name came out funny on my slightly swollen tongue, so I said it again. "Bland-done. Wow, that so works." I giggled and shrugged as I took another bite. "Get it? Because he's bland, and I'm done."

Hawk gave a deep chuckle at my joke, heating my cheeks as I continued to eat the cake. It was quiet for a bit before he asked me a question.

"What would your wedding be like if you chose it?"

"Hmm. Well, for one, it wouldn't be so dang close to my birthday. It's already bad enough to share a day with Valentine's Day *and* spring training most years. But yeah, let's add a wedding anniversary then too. Nope." I shook my head, shoving more cake into my mouth, not caring as I continued to speak. "I'd want the end of summer, the beginning of fall, which of course, will never happen since its playoff season. But that's what I'd want. It's when the sunflowers are in bloom, and there are fields of them. I'd like to get married outside among them, not at a baseball stadium."

"That sounds more like you."

"Thank you." I smiled at him, stopping my cake stuffing. "I'd also like it to be small. Just family and friends. No more than fifty people. I don't care if 'so and so' came and saw me at the hospital one time; I don't want to share my wedding with people who remind me I was once sick."

"I think it's easier for people to see you for who you were and not the beautiful woman you've become."

My fork stopped midway to my mouth, and my eyes landed on his. They were staring at me, no deception hidden in their depths. My cheeks flushed at his praise, and I struggled to know what to say.

"You know, this is the longest we've talked in forever that isn't about baseball. Hell, the most we've hung out since..." I trailed off; the last night that I'd spent any significant time with Hawk coming back to me.

It was the summer after Bryce and Hawk's freshman year of college, and they were both working as bat boys for the Blue Devils. Dad had been the general manager for a few years by then, easily getting them the positions. He wanted to inspire them and reward both of their first seasons at Vanderbilt. They both griped about being too old to be bat boys, even if the age limit was twenty, which they were both still under. But I knew they secretly loved it, especially if the smiles and the way they geeked out at practices were any indication.

Mom and Dad had only been divorced for about a year, and it was my summer with Dad, so I got to join the team for all their games. The Blue Devils gave me odd jobs to help out, from checking press passes, picking out fans to attend VIP signing events, and tracking stats for the players. Anything to keep me busy, really. But I didn't mind. It was fun, and I liked being included for once.

Bryce, Hawk, and I spent most of our time hanging out between and after games since we weren't allowed to attend any afterparties or events. We'd watch movies, play truth or dare, and see how many gross combos of food and drinks we could make. In the grand scheme of things, it was one of the best summers I ever had, probably because my mom wasn't hovering over me every second to check for new bruises.

At some stadiums, they would meet girls and hang out after the game, living the nineteen-year-old lifestyle to its finest. One night toward the middle of the summer, Bryce had a date, but Hawk didn't. The three of us had been having a scary movie marathon, watching all our favorites, and seeing who would scream first.

Earlier that day, Bryce had commented that I wouldn't understand his wanting to hang out with girls instead of his little sister because I hadn't kissed anyone. In little sister fashion, I wanted to leave him out of something, so I convinced Hawk to continue without Bryce.

Midway through the movie, I screamed and turned to cringe at Hawk, expecting him to laugh at me. Instead, I found him staring at me and not watching the movie at all.

"Is it true?"

"What?" I asked, my voice a little breathless. *It's from the movie and not being alone in a room with Hawk.*

"You've never been kissed?"

"Oh. You heard that?" My cheeks instantly flamed. I swallowed, turning back to the movie. *Shit. I must sound so lame.*

"Answer the question, Blazy," he demanded, his voice lower and more of a growl. I could feel his breath on my neck, goosebumps breaking out as I continued to pretend I was watching the movie.

"It's true. Hard to kiss boys when they're all afraid you have some disease they can catch," I mumbled. *Teenage boys were dumb. I had a genetic disorder, not an STI.*

"Blazy."

"Yeah?" I turned my head, and his hand cupped my cheek, our lips fusing together before I knew what was happening. My whole world exploded as Hawk kissed me, taking my breath and gravity altogether.

Of course, thirty seconds later, Bryce returned to the room, and we jumped apart like we hadn't just been making out. My brother had looked at us funny but assumed there was no way what he'd imagined had occurred and dismissed it.

Bryce turned his focus to Hawk, telling him his date had a friend, so they'd returned to grab him to make it a double date.

I'd never seen Hawk move so fast before. He jumped up, and they were both out the door before I could ask them what time they'd be back.

From that point forward, Hawk barely spoke to me alone, basically ignoring me for the rest of the summer. Most of our conversation revolved around politeness, with an occasional inquiry into how the other was doing. I filed it away as my first kiss and let go of my crush on him.

Or so I'd thought.

Looking at him now, I wondered if he even remembered that night. It had been so significant for me, but it had to be one of many kisses for him. I picked at the comforter, my words hanging in the air like an old helium balloon.

"Since the night I kissed you and ran away," he admitted, his voice deep.

Our eyes locked, the air sizzling between us.

"Yeah. That."

I licked my lips, wondering what I was supposed to say.

"It was kind of a dick move."

Okay, so I guess that worked.

Hawk barked out a laugh, rubbing his hand over his shaved head. "Yeah. It was. Sorry." His brows creased, the corner of his lips tilting up in an apologetic smile.

"Apology accepted." I nodded, taking another bite. "So, how's life? Any significant others? Jealous exes? New quirks?"

Hawk chuckled, the tension leaving his face as he shook his head. "No one in the picture. As for exes, they all knew where we stood." He sighed, rubbing his jaw. I could hear the words he wasn't saying.

It's only one night. No-strings sex. Then they get the cleat retreat.

Gulping at the thought, I almost missed his next statement.

"Does having tea parties with my niece count as a quirk?"

I smiled as I pictured Hawk sitting at a little table with a pink teacup. "Definitely. How is Wren? How many kids does she have now?"

Hawk softened as he talked about his sister and nieces, now plural since she just had a baby. It was clear by the way he spoke how much he loved them.

Hawk had become so protective of Wren after their mom's death, hellbent on taking care of her and his dad. I wondered if he realized how amazing he was. Not many people would work so hard for others. It made me want to ensure he had fun. That he took some time for himself and only focused on the now. We could both do with some fun.

"You know what we should do," I said, sitting up and toppling a few containers. The room had grown darker as night fell, casting us into shadows with only the light from the TV. I moved the empty boxes, piling what was left into another.

"What?" he asked, flicking his gaze to mine. "You feeling any more effects?"

"No. I'm fine. You caught it before it became anything. Thanks, by the way."

"It's nothing," he said, sitting up. My eyes immediately went to the expanse of skin that showed as his shirt scrunched up, highlighting his delicious ab muscles. I could just start to see the hint of a V on his hips. Blinking, I shook my head. Both to clear it and dismiss his statement.

"Um, it totally is. I'm shocked you remembered that, actually. Not many people know I'm allergic."

"Yeah, well, I've known you longer than most. I guess it's that big brother energy. It sticks with me."

"Right." My heart sank momentarily at his phrasing, but I decided not to let it settle. We were going to have fun. "Anyway, we need to go swimming."

"Swimming?" he asked, his voice bordering on incredulity as he stared at me, his eyes narrowed. Before I could respond, he answered. "No."

"Fine. I'll just go without you."

Jumping off the bed, the food containers I'd just cleared spilled, but I wouldn't worry about them right now. Lifting the bottle of champagne, I flew out the door and down the hall before he could stop me.

When he caught up to me at the elevator, I smiled over at him and handed him the bottle. I'd already opened it, shocked when it was a twist-off and not corked. *Couldn't even splurge for the good stuff, eh, Mom?*

Sighing like the weight of the world rested on his shoulders, he took it and drank a long swig before handing it back to me. Smirking, I stepped into the elevator, and Hawk followed begrudgingly.

Barefoot, hoodie up, and wearing clothes I didn't own, we rode in silence to the pool, tension and heat swirling between us as excitement built inside me.

It was time for another curve ball.

HAWK

SIX

OF COURSE, she brought up the kiss. The one moment in my life I'd chosen my wants over everyone else. It had been everything I'd thought it would be. For those few minutes that our lips connected, I felt weightless and free.

No little sister to worry about.

No mother to watch over.

No father to impress.

Not even my best friend to stress over.

It was just me and Blazy, and for that pocket of time, she was mine.

But then the door sounded, and reality crashed in.

She was sixteen and my best friend's little sister. If Bryce tried to make a move on Wren, I'd punch him. It didn't matter that he never would, considering she was five years younger than us, and thus fourteen—bro code was bro code. And I'd broken it.

I'd jumped up when he asked and put his needs

before my own, shoving my feelings and dreams of ever being with Blake down deep and locking them away.

And they'd stayed there for nine years.

She wasn't wrong that this was the longest we'd spoken or hung out since then. Ignoring my desire was easier when I wasn't around her. Plus, she'd been dating numbnuts for the past five years. It helped keep her firmly in the unavailable category, even if I hated her boyfriend's guts, which made me hate my comment about the big brother energy. But what did I expect? It had been my intention, after all, to put some space between us. To draw out the boundaries. I should feel thrilled she didn't protest or call me on my bullshit.

But it grated every fiber within me. I didn't want her to think of me as her brother. Not even close.

Turning my head against the back of the elevator, I allowed myself to take her in fully. I'd been a little stunned at how beautiful she'd become earlier when she'd jumped into my car, tear-streaked and in a wedding dress. But seeing her in my clothes, makeup-free, and with her glasses on, stole my fucking breath away.

That small attraction I had toward her all those years ago roared to life, taking on a new shape, and I didn't know if I was strong enough to resist it anymore.

Or if I wanted to.

"You're going to get me in trouble," I grumbled, folding my arms across my chest as I frowned at her.

"Ha! I'm the good girl, Hawk. Haven't you heard? I've never been in trouble my whole life. It's statistically impossible." She smiled over at me, her eyes twinkling with delight and making my cock hard as I imagined calling her, "Good girl."

"Not by my count," I mumbled, following her out of the elevator as it landed on the floor with the pool. "Besides, your brother will murder me if anything happens."

"You worry too much, Hawk. You need to relax."

I snorted, shaking my head. I didn't know what relaxed was.

"This isn't you, Blazy."

"Yeah? Well, maybe it should be. I'm sick of playing it safe. Today I finally made a decision for myself, and it felt good. Why should I stop?"

She'd halted suddenly in the hallway and turned, her body pressing into mine as she spoke. Her cheeks became a perfect shade of rose, traveling down her neck, and I couldn't help but shamelessly follow the path with my eyes, wishing I could see how far it went. Swallowing, my Adam's apple bobbed as I clenched my fists to avoid touching her. Lust and desire blazed to life between us.

There's more at stake now than ever.

But my cock refused to listen, growing harder each second she was pressed against me, her apple smell mixing with my cologne to create the most intoxicating scent ever. Even better than baseball.

When I said nothing, she spun around, and her bare feet continued their trek down the hallway. I took a moment to groan into my fist as I watched her ass sway, wondering what the hell I'd been thinking about giving her my shorts to wear.

Blake opened the door to the pool, the smell of chlorine tumbling out into the hall and clearing my nostrils of us. She paused before she stepped through, turning back to look at me.

"Don't make me pull out the dares," she challenged, lifting her eyebrows.

"Ha! I do believe I'm still the reigning dare champ," I retorted, my feet moving before I could think twice. It wasn't like I could let her go in there alone. I was just making sure she was safe.

Yeah, I didn't buy it either, but it assuaged my guilt for not stopping her as I stepped into the humid room. It was empty and dark, the pool hours having ended an hour ago. It was both a relief and a fear.

At least no one else would see Blake in her underwear, but the fear of getting caught and kicked out had my blood pumping. I could see the scandal the tabloids would paint already.

"Runaway bride, baseball's darling daughter, skinny dips with the trailer trash catcher hours after leaving her groom at the altar."

Not that I was trailer trash anymore, but some things were hard to wash off, and the media liked to remind me where I'd crawled my ass out of.

Some things were better left at the trailer park, and my past was one of them.

Blake pulled the hoodie and shirt over her head, stopping my mercurial thoughts as I sucked in a breath at her sheer bra thing. She pushed the shorts down next, stealing another of my breaths as I took her in, wearing nothing but her bra and panties.

Fuck me.

Blake took another swig of champagne before leaving it on a table. Peering over her shoulder, she gave me a wink as she took off her glasses, sat them on top of the pile, and dove into the deep end.

Where did all of this confidence come from? Not that I was complaining. I loved seeing her full of sass and light. It was the way Blake was meant to be, a full blaze. Now that I saw it in full force, I could see how much she'd dulled over the past five years.

I might've avoided her, but I'd kept tabs on her in the periphery out of brotherly concern.

Yeah, I was only fooling myself.

She lifted out of the water, the liquid sluicing over her skin as she propped her arms on the side. I would've thought this whole evening was a scheme if it had been any other woman. But it was Blake. She didn't know how to lie or manipulate. It wasn't in her to be disingenuous. Add in the fact I knew she was a virgin, and I had to assume she had no idea the temptress she was.

How had the bland numbnuts kept it in his pants for five years? His nuts had to be really numb.

"You coming?"

I choked out a cough at her words as my head went fuzzy. Fucking hell. She was going to kill me. I wasn't sure if I even cared.

Blake pushed off from the side and floated on her back, exposing her breasts as they peeked above the water, her perfect nipples showing through the wet fabric.

Shit. Fuck. Dammit. I was going to hell.

"I didn't take the rebel backstop of KC to be such a stick in the mud," she taunted, pulling out the name the crowd liked to call me, proving she followed at least some of my games.

Why did I like that so much?

All of my willpower fled at her words, and there was no other recourse for me as I kicked off my shoes and pulled the shirt over my head. Tugging my sweat-pants, I prayed my boxers concealed my raging erection as I cannonballed near her, splashing water all over her cute face. She shrieked and laughed, splashing me back as I surfaced.

"You better swim fast, Blazy," I warned a second before I dove for her.

My arms wrapped around her torso thirty seconds later, and I carried her with me as I swam, trapping her against the deep end wall when we emerged.

"No fair, you didn't give me a real chance," she sassed, slapping my chest.

Water clung to her eyelashes, her blue eyes bright as she tried to argue her case. Her legs had naturally wrapped around my body, her arms perched on my own.

It took every shred of respect I had for Bryce not to rock into her.

"Fine. You have one more shot. But if I catch you, I'm hauling your ass back to the room. You had your swim. We need to get out of her before someone realizes we're in here after hours."

"Spoilsport," she teased, smiling at me.

I fixed my glare; my eyes narrowed as I waited for her to acquiesce.

"Fine, Grumpy Gramps. But give me a five-second head start. I want a fair chance."

"I'll give you eight because I'm kind like that. Eight," I started, holding in my laugh as her eyes widened, and she struggled to get out of my arms and swim away as I continued to count. "Seven, six, five, four."

Holding her breath, she gave up pushing my arms away and went under the water, swimming away from me.

"Three, two, one!" I shouted, diving under the water. Luckily, I had the advantage over her of being able to see underwater, though it wasn't a significant one with how dark it was. I turned back and forth as I searched for her, bubbles trailing up as I spent my oxygen. Just before I needed to surface, I caught sight of movement off to the left side.

Pushing up, I sucked in a large breath before ducking back under the water and swam in the direction I'd last seen her. As I neared, she came more into focus. When she spotted me, she laughed, losing her oxygen and surfacing as she continued to swim away from me.

Her panties and bra were even more translucent underwater, and I groaned as I got a full view of her nearly naked body. I wrapped my arms around her and broke through the water with my prize in tow.

"Got you." I smiled at her, triumph and joy bubbling in me. This was what Blake did. She made everything fun. I'd missed it more than I'd known, falling into my 'Grumpy Gramps' persona as she teased me about, the longer I avoided her.

"Fine, you win," she whined but followed it with a laugh. "You can't deny it wasn't fun, though. I've liked seeing your smile." Her hands cupped my face as her fingers traced over my lips.

It was intimate, reminding me how close our bodies were and how few layers were between us. I couldn't stop myself this time as I rocked up, her eyes rolling back as she gasped. Her mouth opened as her head fell back against the edge, and she tightened her legs, rocking herself against me this time, her fingers digging into my biceps.

Groaning, I dropped my head to her shoulder, praying for strength.

Her fingers moved, running through my hair, her nails biting into my scalp, sending shivers through me, and breaking the laser-thin shred of control I had left.

"Goddamn, Blazy. What are you doing to me?" I gasped, despite knowing full well.

"Me?" She chuckled, the sound husky and deep as she continued her ministrations in my hair, her hips slowly rolling against me. It was pleasure and torture wrapped together. "I believe you're the one who rocked the anaconda trapped in your briefs into me first."

I lifted my head and met her eyes. Her pupils were blown, her eyes darker than I'd ever seen them, making the blue almost navy. My thumb traced over her cheek, her eyes fluttering closed at my touch.

"You're so goddamn beautiful. I'm not right for you at all. I can't give you all the things you deserve." God, but I wanted to. If there was ever a woman I would give up everything for, it was her, but I couldn't. Not yet. People still needed me. Plus, there was the complication of Bryce. If I was going to be with his sister, I owed him the courtesy of talking to him about it.

"What if I just want tonight? I want to feel good, Hawk. *Please*. Make me feel good. You were my first kiss. Be my other first, too."

Her plea shredded my heart in two. Of course, I was only good for one night. But I was too weak to deny her. If this was my chance to be with her, I'd take it even if it killed something inside me. I could wallow in how much her words cut me later, but I'd focus on making this good for her right now.

My right hand skimmed down her stomach as her body trembled in my arms. I kept her eyes locked with mine as I brushed my knuckle across her pelvic bone. She whimpered, moving her hips forward to find more friction.

Growling, I took both of her hands in my free one and trapped them against the edge of the pool, thankful we'd swam to the shallow end as I braced my feet on the ground. I had her trapped against the wall, my body pressed into hers, and her arms secured. She looked so fucking perfect that I couldn't hold back any longer as I sank a finger into her.

The second I entered her warm channel, stars exploded behind my eyes as I watched her buck against me, her body responding to what I was doing to her. Blake's legs stayed around my waist as I thrust my finger in and out, her gasps of pleasure edging me on as I sealed our lips together.

Both of us had come a long way in the kissing department in nine years. Her tongue rolled over mine, not shy as she sought entrance into my mouth. Her hips continued to buck as she pulled against my hold. Pleasure, unlike anything I'd ever experienced, slammed into me, and I had to recite all thirty baseball teams in the Majors backward and forward to stop myself from exploding in the pool.

Flicking my thumb against her clit, I felt the instant she came undone. Her walls tightened around my digit, trapping it inside as warmth wrapped around me. Her body trembled as she rode out her orgasm, and I swallowed her moan as she came.

Blinking open her eyes, I pulled back as I released my grip. I didn't know if she'd want more or if she'd freak out now that the lust had left her. I froze in place as I waited for her response. This would either end a lifelong friendship or be the most incredible night of my life.

"More. I want more. Fuck me, Hawk. Take my virginity and make me yours."

There weren't enough cuss words to express the level of fuckery in my mind as I kissed her, tangling her tongue with mine as I lifted us out of the water, somehow making it to our pile of clothes.

Laughing, we dried off haphazardly and pulled the dry clothes over us, but neither of us could keep our hands off one another now that we'd opened that door. Stumbling out of the pool, we returned to the elevator without running into anyone in the hall, our secret pool rendezvous remaining under wraps.

A couple gave us knowing looks when we stepped onto the elevator but kept quiet, exiting two floors before us and allowing my lips to return to Blake's as I lifted her into my arms.

The only thing that would stop me now was a natural disaster.

Blake

SEVEN

I PINCHED MYSELF, worried another recurring nightmare was happening. One where I would get clam-jammed anytime I was about to have sex—real or imaginary. I'd often dreamed of Hawk in this position, only to have my mother or brother rush into the room and whisk me away.

"What are you doing?" Hawk asked, narrowing his eyes at my fingers as he approached, the door locking behind him.

"Making sure this isn't a dream," I mumbled, my breathing increasing as the tension between us doubled.

My whole body was taut with need, the earlier remnants of the orgasm at the edges as I recalled how Hawk had made me tremble. I'd never felt that before. And now that I had, I wanted more.

Large, rough hands grasped my face and tilted it upward.

"You dream about me, Blazy?"

"*Yes*," I admitted shamelessly. It came out sounding more like a moan than an answer.

Hawk smirked, his lips twitching up on one side, and his mismatched eyes looked like molten lava, ready to boil over, heating every square inch of my skin and encasing us in a tomb of our own making.

Surprisingly, I didn't mind that imagery—us wrapped up together for eternity. *Yes, please.*

Hawk gripped the bottom of the hoodie and raised it, pulling it over my head. I suddenly felt the urge to yell out everything embarrassing that entered my head—I was clam-jamming myself now.

"Did you steal my pin?"

He stopped his movements, which unfortunately meant my head was covered, and my breasts were on display in my wet bra.

"Um, what?" he asked, clearing his throat. Hawk tugged the hoodie the rest of the way off my head, allowing me to see my surroundings again.

"Nothing." I shook my head, deciding to shut up for once. I reached back and unhooked my bra, tossing the sodden material to the side.

"Hot damn," Hawk groaned, staring at my breasts. I didn't think they were anything special, but with how he looked at them, it made me feel sexy. Biting my lip, I pushed my borrowed shorts and wet panties down, stepping out of them as I stood up straight, completely naked.

Channeling the sexiness Hawk inspired in me, I turned and crawled onto the bed, purposefully taunting him with my bare ass as I settled down. There were still a few empty boxes, so I pushed them to the side and rested on my elbows as I brazenly parted my legs.

"You're not going to back out now, are you?" I taunted. Inside, I was shaking, my nerves overwhelming me as I waited for him to decide. I didn't know if I could handle the rejection if he changed his mind after seeing me naked.

A primal groan fell from his lips as he tore his shirt off his body, kicking the shoes and sweats to the side as he stalked to the bed. I gulped as I took in the large member between his legs; the behemoth was hard and thick as he approached.

I didn't get to look much longer as my thighs were wrenched apart and my ass lifted in the air. My arms fell back as my body gave way to gravity, distracting me from Hawk and his mission momentarily. When his hot mouth landed on my pussy, I bucked and gasped at the shock. His eyes danced as he held me to his mouth like his favorite snack.

My thighs sat on his shoulders, the majority of my body now off the bed as he licked and sucked me. Gasping, my fingers searched for something to claw at as blood rushed to my head from the angle he held me. So many sensations fired within me that my brain was overwhelmed, struggling to know what to focus on next.

Brandon had attempted oral once after a lot of begging on my part, but it hadn't been anything like this. I wasn't sure if he'd just sucked at it or intentionally made it unpleasant so he wouldn't have to do it again. It was obvious now that he hadn't liked it. Not if it had felt so underwhelming.

Because everything Hawk did set my blood on fire, my heart racing, and my head spinning. I couldn't tell up from down, but knew I never wanted him to stop. It felt that damn good. He was a magician with his tongue as he licked and sucked my clit.

"Holy… Oh… Yes… Hawk!" I screamed, not even capable of forming complete sentences. His sharp stubble rubbed against my inner thigh as he pulled back, his face glistening as he stuck out his tongue, licking his lips. My breath caught in my throat as I watched, completely enraptured. *Damn, that was sexy.*

"You taste divine, Blake. I could eat you all day long and never grow tired of your pussy. Your legs belong wrapped around my head, my face nestled in your soaking wet cunt."

My body shuddered at his words. No man had ever spoken such filth to me before. But I couldn't deny how much wetter it made me. How much I wanted to hear him say more. How much I wish it was true.

"Please," I whimpered, squirming as I tried to get a better purchase, needing more friction.

Hawk's smirk turned into a full grin as he held my gaze, distracting me from his next trick. Plunging his fingers into me, my body arched, and I instantly spasmed around them as he flicked my clit with his tongue, sucking it into his mouth.

"Ah, yes!"

"Give me it all, baby," he purred, spurring me on. I couldn't even attempt to be self-conscious as I orgasmed, my moans loud as I came undone. Hawk bit the inner side of my left thigh, giving me something to focus on; that tiny bit of pain kept me conscious as he pumped his fingers faster and deeper, curving them up until I crashed through another orgasm. At some point, my body returned to the bed, my bones weightless as I melted into the mattress.

"I knew you'd blush so prettily here," he whispered, dragging his finger down my body. I felt him as he traveled the valley between my breasts, his fingers brushing against the small scar on my sternum. He circled my belly button and then touched my hip bones, touching those scars, too. They were tiny and silver, barely noticeable to most people. But I was learning Hawk wasn't most people. He seemed to notice everything.

His hand returned, cupping my jaw as he peered into my eyes. I tried to stare into his to figure out what he was feeling or thinking, but this close, I kept having to bounce back and forth between the hazel and ice blue one, making it impossible to decipher.

"Kiss me," I begged, no longer caring how desperate I sounded. I pulled his face to mine, my fingers scraping against his scalp. I wanted to memorize everything about him and sear it onto my soul. I wrapped my leg around him, bringing his cock closer. Feeling it rub against me, I moaned into the kiss, needy for more.

Hell, I never felt this horny or lust drunk for Brandon.

Hawk broke the kiss and pulled back, watching me

from his higher position. His chest moved up and down, his breath coming in choppy spurts as he seared his eyes into me. It made me feel incredibly powerful to think I was affecting him, even if only an iota of how crazy he made me feel.

Hawk fisted his cock, his eyes never leaving me. I trailed mine down, taking in his tattoos. There were about five on his chest that I wanted to trace with my tongue, but when I got to the bee under his left pec, I froze.

"We can stop if you've changed your mind," he said, his voice strained. I flicked my gaze back up, the rejection and vulnerability in his eyes hitting me in my chest like a large anvil. Swallowing, I shook my head.

"No. I want this. I'm ready." My eyes held his, showing how much I meant it. Finally, he nodded and leaned over me to grab a foil wrapper off the night-stand. Had that been there all along? My questions ground to a halt as I watched in amazement as he rolled it on, his cock thick and long as it strained against the latex. Licking my lips, I leaned up, wishing I'd tasted him first.

"It's going to hurt at first, baby. I tried to relax you as much as I could so it wouldn't feel as bad, but there's no getting around the bit of pain. Just breathe through it, and then it will feel good again. I promise."

"I trust you," I said, meaning it.

Something shifted in his gaze at my words, and he notched himself at my entrance, his muscles tight as he braced himself. Ever so slowly, he moved, and I watched as he pushed his cock in. The feeling of wholeness was immediate, and I arched my back, wanting, no, *needing* more of him. His cock was hard as granite and warm, spreading and stretching me in ways I hadn't known were possible.

It felt unlike anything I could've imagined.

My fingers. His fingers. My dildos. None of them were authentic replacements for the real thing. Not even close.

Because, holy hell, his dick felt good. There was some pain as he continued to push in, but the feeling of being filled sent tingles through me, my body buzzing as it came to life. Something in me clicked, and I wrapped my legs around him, needing him further inside me. It wasn't enough.

Sucking in a breath as the sharp twinge of pain increased, I clawed at his back as I rolled through it, trying to take deep breaths like he said. When there didn't feel like any more space could be between us, he stopped, his body pressed tight against mine. His hands cupped my cheeks as he peered at me.

"You okay?"

"Mmhmm." I bit my lip as I squirmed. I needed to move or shift or flex my walls. When I did all three, his eyes rolled back as my pussy clenched tighter around him.

"Shit, Blazy. You already feel fucking amazing. I'm barely hanging on by a thread, and then you go and do *that*. Do you want to see me go feral?" he growled.

"*Yes*," I groaned, arching my back to rub my nipples

against his chest. Nothing in the world had ever sounded as good as Hawk Anderson going feral on me.

"Move! Fuck me with your big dick," I ordered.

Hawk gave a dark chuckle, squeezing my thigh in his hand. "Such a dirty mouth for a sweet girl. I might need to wash it out later with my cum."

Before I could retort something sarcastic, he finally moved, shifting his hips forward and hitting me deeper than before. My eyes rolled back as he undulated his hips into me, his cock moving in and out with each thrust and hitting me deep. My hands roamed over his back, his muscles flexing against my fingers as I gripped his ass, clawing at him as I tried to pull him into me even more.

He was right. Now that the pain had gone, it felt fucking incredible. My head was a mess of fuzziness as I chased the volcano building inside me. It started at my spine, my limbs tingling as it raced through me like hot lava, the hair on my neck standing up as goosebumps spread; I moaned and groaned, sounding like an amateur porn star as I moved my hips in rhythm with Hawk.

I didn't know what I was doing, but my body seemed to have an instinctual connection to Hawk, moving effortlessly with him.

His thrusts picked up, and the sound of skin slapping mingled with our groans. I didn't know where I ended, and he began; we were one as we moved, my arms wrapped around his head and my legs his waist. If we fell through the bed to the floor below us or if the world burned down around us, I wouldn't know because I could only feel, hear, and see Hawk. *He was everywhere.*

His hands were on me. His cock in me. His lips left lingering grazes on my neck. I was addicted to how he moaned and how his breath fell from his lips in little puffs as he gave himself over to me. The feeling of his beard against every sensitive part of my body would forever be imprinted on my skin. The only sensations I felt were of him, and I didn't know how I'd survive this when it was over.

I knew it was only one night, that it was all he could offer, and then the real cleat retreat would occur. Not the one Bryce mentioned earlier, but this, right here. Because I wanted so much more with him, from him.

He wrote his name on my heart with each thrust, leaving his mark behind. It might only be my virginity to him, but to me, Hawk was changing my life, altering the very core of who I was. This connection was so much more than a one-night stand. There was no way this was what sex felt like with strangers, with the ball girls and cleat chasers. Even sex with Brandon would've never felt like *this*, and I firmly believed now that sex should always be like this. Sex with Hawk had awoken something inside me, and I was a glutton for it.

My whole body was in sync with his, moving and grinding as I became weightless. The only thing I knew was pleasure as Hawk pistoned in me, stealing my very breath from me as I let go of everything and gave it all to him.

Stars teased the corners of my eyes as my head fell back, my vision going dark as the orgasm crashed over me, sending wave after wave through me. I trembled with release as his cock kept pushing in, sending aftershocks through me, and I barely held back the words that wanted to spill from me.

Be mine forever.

Somewhere in the recesses of my mind, I knew I'd made the right decision to walk away from Brandon. There was no way I could go back to being a vacant husk of myself after this.

When Hawk tensed, I watched as he came. His eyes held mine, no masks between us as his mouth opened, a moan escaping as he jerked inside me, his hips moving in short bouts. When he finished, he dropped to the side, just staring at me.

I didn't know what he was thinking, but I hoped it was the same as me.

This might've started as a rebound, a way to pass the time and check off something I'd been holding onto for far too long.

But it had been right. Perfect even.

It would be messy and complicated, but he was worth it. I'd deal with Bryce and my parents if I got to be his.

"You okay?" he asked after we'd both been quiet for a while.

"Better than okay. How many condoms do you have?" I asked, sitting up.

"A few more. Why?" He quirked his brow, watching me with curiosity.

I climbed off the bed, grabbed the cake box and fork, and sat back on the bedspread naked as I smiled.

"Because we're *so* doing that again." I forked a piece of cake, shoved it in his mouth as he chuckled, and then did the same for myself. "There are a bunch more positions I want to try. That was the best thing I've ever experienced, and I'm not ready to stop yet. Are you?" I asked, holding out another bite.

He stared at me, searching for something. In that second, he looked the most vulnerable I'd ever seen. Gone was the Hawk with the weight of the world on his shoulders, looking older than he was. In his place was a bright-eyed boy, letting himself be free for once. We'd both been stuck in our roles. I'd never seen it before, but it was plain as day now that my eyes were open. I stopped and cupped his cheek, swiping my thumb across it.

He stilled, peering at me, waiting for something. I just kept hold of his cheek, pouring everything I felt into my look. His hand came up and covered mine, and this time it was his eyes that bounced between my two blue ones. Hawk swallowed before the most beautiful smile spread across his face, setting butterflies racing around me as my heart flipped over.

Damn, that might've been better than the orgasm.

"Oh, Blazy. There are so many things I want to show you. You won't be able to walk straight when I'm done."

He leaped up, tackling me back to the bed, not caring that icing and cake were now all over us. Though, when he licked it off my chest a few minutes later, I didn't care either.

Mmm. Sex and cake. The absolute best combo.

Blake

EIGHT

LYING IN BED, I realized my muscles ached in a way I'd never experienced before. Because I'd been sick most of my childhood, I hadn't been allowed to do many physical activities. But even after the bone marrow transplant, my mom had become so hyper-focused on ensuring I was well that I still wasn't allowed to do anything that might wear me out.

But now, each way I moved, I could feel the pull of muscles I hadn't known existed. It was a soreness that spoke of great adventures and triumph. As I rested against Hawk's body, his arm draped over my half-naked body, I couldn't help but smile at the sensation.

Everything hurt, and I loved it.

Sighing in bliss, I snuggled back into Hawk's warmth as I debated if there was still time to try one more position before anyone came to look for me. I knew I should feel guilty for ghosting everyone, but I couldn't find it in me to turn my phone back on. Bryce said he'd handle it, and I trusted him to do just that. He'd always taken care of me, and I knew he'd swoop in with his big brother energy for this, too.

I should probably look at how often he rescued me. But later.

"Don't tell me you're a morning person, Blazy," Hawk grumbled behind me, his breath tickling my neck.

Smiling, I rolled over and ran my hands over his bare chest, tracing his tattoos. At some point, Hawk had made us both put on some form of clothing to put a barrier between us. It was his attempt to persuade us to keep our hands to ourselves.

It hadn't worked the way he intended.

The man looked sexy in gray sweatpants. Especially when he didn't have anything on under them. Apparently, I looked just as irresistible in his t-shirt, so I guess it was a fair playing field.

"And what if I am?" I teased, grinning.

"Hmm. I'll have to rethink this."

"*This*?" I asked, my voice hitching. I'd hoped it could be more, wanted it more than anything, but I knew the pitfalls. Hawk was Bryce's best friend, and it was clear where I stood in that dynamic. Plus, Hawk hadn't ever had a serious girlfriend before. Why would he change that for me? I'd told myself I was fine with one night. That it was better than nothing.

But now… hope springs eternal and all that crap.

My body tingled with anticipation as I waited for what he would say.

He cracked open one eye, the ice-blue color searing into me. "I'm not sure what you think about me and how I treat women, but I don't go around sticking my dick in just anything."

"Wow. So romantic," I deadpanned.

Hawk narrowed his eye at me, and goosebumps raised along my skin. I could already hear the possessive growl in his voice, even when he didn't say anything.

"And here I thought you were the king of one-night stands with a heave-ho the next morning. Bryce even has a word for it. Said you coined it."

Hawk turned on his side, hovering over me and trapping me with his body as his eyes simmered like molten lava.

"I don't give a fuck what Bryce said. I'm telling you the score. Do you hear me?"

I nodded, but the freedom to speak my mind with Hawk flooded out of me before I could stop it.

"Oh, I heard you all night long as you screamed out my name. Maybe I'm the queen of one-night stands," I chirped, my cheeks heating at my taunt.

Hawk's eyes darkened, his pupils so blown I could barely make out any color. He leaned forward until our noses touched.

"We might be out of condoms, baby, but I still haven't taught you what I can do to that smart mouth of yours. Call yourself the queen of one-night stands again and see how that works out for you."

Eek! I pressed my lips together, my eyes heating at the thought. Why did I want to test him?

The left corner of his mouth crept up, his stubble more pronounced today. I lifted my hand and ran it over the sharp edges. My body bore the marks of his beard, rubbing me in all the places, branding me as his.

"But Bryce…" I said, leaving it at that.

Hawk let out a deep breath. "Yeah. I know. I'll—"

A loud noise interrupted him as a door I hadn't noticed in the middle of the wall smacked against the dresser as it opened.

"Hawk! You in here, bruh? I've been trying to get a hold of you. Have you seen Blake?" my brother asked as he stepped through from the adjoining room.

We jumped apart and sprang up as his head lifted, his eyes widening as he took in the scene before him. I quickly smoothed my hair down as I glanced around the room. In his need to clean, Hawk had taken out all the food boxes, hung our wet clothes in the shower, and tidied up the other things I'd brought into the room sometime between round three or four of sexcapades. So the room didn't look as bad as it would have.

Bryce's eyes widened at the two of us in bed together, but then he dropped his shoulders and smiled as his whole body relaxed. It seemed his relief at finding me outweighed the logic of why we'd be half-dressed side-by-side together.

"BB! There you are. I've been trying to call you all night…" he trailed off, glancing around as his brain caught up and put the pieces together for him. It had to be that he'd been up most of the night dealing with my wedding sham that he hadn't gotten there sooner.

"Wait…" Bryce narrowed his eyes as he stared at his best friend.

"I can explain," Hawk said, sounding guilty as hell. But he froze, half extended out of the bed as the rest of his words died on his tongue.

My thoughts tumbled around as I tried to think of a way to explain this. My eyes caught on the cake topper in the middle of the table, my dress placed delicately over the chair next to it. Outside of us in bed together, which we were both at least dressed this time—thank you, Hawk—I didn't see anything that would infer we'd been fucking one another's brains out.

Time to try to lie to my brother.

"Someone start talking," Bryce demanded, crossing his arms over his chest. I had no doubt if it had been anyone other than Hawk in bed with me, he would've already swung first and asked questions later. His best friend made him pause before jumping to conclusions. But just barely, if the anger radiating off him was anything to go by.

"You see, I was upset, and we ate cake and then nightmares," I rambled, none of it making sense. I had never been a good liar, especially to Bryce.

"Cake?" Bryce asked, blinking as he looked at me, my nonsense making the anger dissipate slightly.

"Yup. The wedding cake." I pointed to the table where the topper was.

Then I saw it.

I'd just pointed my brother right to the one piece of incriminating evidence.

The edge of a gold and black wrapper peeked out from under my dress, where it had fallen in haste as Hawk fucked me against that table. I swallowed, praying Bryce wouldn't see it. But now that I had, I couldn't quit looking at it.

Bryce snorted as he took in the cake toppers. He walked over, my heart beating quicker as he neared the condom wrapper. Picking up the superhero and the '50s housewife, he laughed as he held them before placing them back on the table.

"Why do I feel like breaking out into *Grease Lightnin'* all of a sudden?" he asked with a smile on his face, leaning back against the table.

In a series of unfortunate events—that could only happen to me the morning after losing my virginity to my brother's best friend after I ran away from my wedding—Bryce's leaning shifted my dress, exposing the condom wrapper in all its black and gold glory.

Magnum.

That word would forever be imprinted in my brain as the thing that crashed my chance at happiness.

In slow motion, Bryce bent over and picked it up like he thought it might be a joke condom wrapper. He turned it over and then back to Hawk. My brother's face morphed into one I'd never seen before as his lips thinned, his brows dipped, and his eyes became pinpoints as rage took over.

Quicker than I could blink, he reared his hand back

and punched Hawk in the face. His head whipped around at the force, but he did nothing to stop it. Hawk's shoulders slumped in resignation as he took it.

I screamed in alarm, tears pricking my eyes as I tried to jump between them. This wasn't how I wanted this morning to go. But now that we were here, I had to do something. I couldn't let it all fall apart.

"How could you?" Bryce screamed, shaking his hand, and I worried he'd hurt himself. "She's my baby sister, dude. What happened to bro code?"

"It's not like that, Bry."

Bryce scoffed, shaking his head. "Fucking my sister when she's the most vulnerable is low. I thought you had better morals than that."

Ouch.

It didn't matter that it had taken us both to cross the line; Bryce only blamed Hawk. For their friendship and my heart, I couldn't let Hawk or Bryce ruin that. I could see that now. Bryce would never accept this—Hawk and me. So, I did the only thing I could; I gave my brother the transplant he needed to survive.

Except instead of bone marrow, I'd give him my heart.

"It was all me, Bry. I got him drunk and took advantage of him. I told Hawk that if he didn't, I'd go down to the bar and bring back the first person I ran into."

Hawk moved to stop me, his eyes hard as he stared at me, urging me to shut up and let him handle it. But I couldn't do that. So I turned to him, holding his mismatched eyes and knowing I had to ensure he understood. It was the only way.

"It meant nothing. Just one night of fun between two friends." The words were hollow and tasted bitter on my lips. I turned back to my brother, fighting back the tears that wanted to fall. "It's not a thing, Bry. I promise. He broke no bro code or whatever. You're best friends. Don't ruin that over nothing."

"*Nothing*," Hawk said like the word gutted him, leaving him empty.

It was only because Bryce looked from me to Hawk that I could shut my eyes as my body shuddered at that word. It felt like my heart had just been shattered.

"BB took advantage of you?" Bryce asked. I didn't think he believed the lie, but it was easier for him to accept it instead of losing his best friend.

"I barely remember anything," Hawk said, his voice low and emotionless. His eyes had gone cold, and I curled my fingers inward to stop myself from reaching out to him. To touch him. To soothe him. *To love him.*

"Fucking hell," Bryce wheezed, sitting in the spare chair. He braced his arms on his knees and tugged at the ends of his hair as he took a deep breath. I took a chance to glance at Hawk. But he wouldn't look at me. Bryce finally looked up, grimacing as he took in Hawk's cheek, which was now swelling.

"Shit. I'm sorry, man. I've barely slept, and when I couldn't reach either of you, I got nervous. It's been hell dealing with the parentals, and then I discovered fucking *Olson* got traded to the Blue Devils. He's taking my old spot."

It was then I realized I'd gone almost a whole day without baseball being the center of conversation.

"Fuck, man. What was your dad thinking?" Hawk asked, moving further away from me as he talked to his best friend.

Bryce sighed, slumping back into the chair, looking utterly defeated. He ping-ponged back and forth between us before he spoke again.

"I still don't like this, but I guess I can deal with it if you both promise it's nothing more. I don't think I could handle that. I just… I never want to have to choose between you two. I need you both in my life." He shook his head, his eyes wild.

"Promise," I said, the words killing me and adding to the guilt as I realized how much I'd placed on him.

"Sorry for the…" He motioned to Hawk's face.

"Don't even worry about it, man. I deserved it." Hawk and Bryce grasped forearms in some bro-slap, apparently the gesture for forgiveness in dude-speak.

"Come on. Let's get something for that eye before it swells so much you can't see, and then I'm accused of spring training sabotage."

"Like you could hurt my game," Hawk scoffed, standing and sliding on his shoes. He grabbed a shirt from his suitcase and headed to the door, his eyes never looking at me.

"We'll get some breakfast and figure out how to handle the rest of this mess, Blanket. Stay put." Bryce kissed my forehead and moved around me, leaving me sitting on the bed in a numb state of emotions.

"Shit, I forgot my key. Grab the elevator. I'll be right there," I heard Hawk say two seconds before he was in front of me, grasping my cheeks and kissing me like I was the air he breathed. It was over just as fast as he grabbed the keycard and jogged to the door.

I sucked in a breath, my heart beating hard in my chest as the tears fell. Hawk paused halfway through the door, his eyes finally connecting with mine, the emotion there a whirlwind behind his mismatched hues.

I saw all the hopes and dreams for a future together race through them in a matter of seconds, making my heart race and wishing I could take my words back.

Then Hawk blinked, and it was gone, replaced with a blankness that left me chilled to the bone as he stepped out the door. The latch clicked shut, the sound striking me in the chest as the best thing to ever happen to me walked away.

Looks like I got the cleat retreat in the end, anyway.

It had to happen.

I knew that. But it didn't make it hurt any less.

Neither of us could lose Bryce, and I wouldn't make my brother choose. He'd given me life once, and now… we were even.

The hard part was I didn't know if I could live without my heart.

Blake

NINE

WITH BROKEN SOBS, I hurried around the room as I gathered my belongings. I couldn't be here when they got back. I just couldn't do it. After everything that happened in the last twenty-four hours, I didn't have it in me to fake that I was okay.

I needed some space from Hawk. It was too fresh, too real. Now that I knew what it felt like to touch him, kiss him, and hold him… it would be torture to hold back.

Thankfully, I'd had the good fortune of packing clean underwear, so I wouldn't have to go commando, and my bra was now dry in the bathroom. Unfortunately, I didn't have any spare clothes. Staring at the wedding dress, I sighed when I knew what I had to do. Back into this ridiculous ensemble. I wasn't even going to try to button it, though. I wasn't that flexible.

Wearing hot pink high tops, a stolen black hoodie—it was mine now—and a wedding dress, I ran out of the side of a building for the second time in twenty-four hours.

Except this time, there was no car waiting for me. I was on my own.

The February wind whipped around me as I walked down the street, storefronts blurring as I passed. I had no idea where I was going, just that I couldn't be in that hotel a moment longer.

The realization this was the first time I'd been alone in months was shattering. I didn't know if I'd been making the best decisions so far, but at least they'd been mine. That was saying something.

A door opened before me, and a girl with teal hair exited. Music from inside blared out into the street, catching my attention. It was an old '90s song.

"I'm a bitch, I'm a lover, I'm a…"

I turned toward it like a siren song instead of continuing my aimless journey. A girl with face piercings and a neck tattoo looked up as I approached, her eyes widening at the bottom half of my outfit.

"Looks like there's a story there," she said in lieu of a greeting, her voice smoky and deep.

"You have no idea." I looked around at the colorful art adorning the wall and the neon lights. "Tattoos," I said as I read the word twisted in neon.

"Yep. And piercings," she said, drawing my attention back. "I should advise you against making an emotional decision, but I have a feeling you need to see this through. Whatever it is."

I snorted, liking that she wasn't dismissing me despite my obvious turmoil.

"Can you tattoo anything?" I asked as an idea formed.

"Just about. What you got in mind, sugar?"

I lifted my dress to show my thigh where Hawk had bitten me, marking me as his right on the inner part of my thigh. For some reason, it felt significant, and I suddenly wanted to immortalize it forever.

"This?" I asked, glancing up. She peered over the counter, tilting her head as she debated.

"Yeah. I can do that. That all?"

"And a hawk."

"Sure, thang. You have a picture?" she asked as she passed over a clipboard with a piece of paper attached. I liked how she rolled with me and accepted my requests as genuine. I hadn't had many people treat me like that. Just how much had I let my mother shelter me?

"Do you have some options?" I asked, scanning the consent form and signing it. I handed her my ID and credit card as she pulled out a book. While she entered the information, I flipped through the portfolio until I found the one I wanted.

Sitting in a chair ten minutes later with my wedding dress hiked up and spilling off to one side, I closed my eyes as the tears fell. It wasn't because of the tattoo gun but the pain in my heart.

"Some people find it cathartic to talk while I'm doing this. Tell me, what's the story behind your attire?

Unless you often wear wedding dresses that cost more than most people's cars." She lifted a brow, and I blushed at that. I hadn't known.

I couldn't blame my ignorance, though. For too long, I'd been walking around numb, letting everyone else make decisions for me and live my life. While I could be mad at them for doing it, I hadn't stopped them either.

This dress proved it, and it was time to take responsibility for the half-life I'd been living.

"Hmm, where to start? I accepted a proposal from a guy I didn't love because I was too scared to say no in front of a crowd of people. Then I convinced myself it would be okay, but when I stood in front of the mirror yesterday, I knew I couldn't go through with it."

"So, you ran away?" she asked, tracing the bite mark.

Smiling, I spent the next however long giving the tale of how I'd run out of the baseball stadium in my high tops. Stolen my own wedding feast by threatening a server with a fork and the ludicrousness of the wedding toppers.

"No shit. Your mom had you as Sandy? Like from *Grease*?" one of the other patrons asked. He was a burly man with several tattoos, sitting a booth over. It was endearing he knew the musical.

"Yep, or at least it resembled her. It was very '50s-esque. Ridiculous, right?"

"That's some messed up shit. What happened next?" another tattoo artist asked.

My cheeks blushed as I thought about swimming and pressuring Hawk to pop my cherry.

"Oh, now comes the good part," Roxie, my tattoo artist, teased, noticing my heated cheeks.

"I might've come on to my brother's best friend," I admitted, dropping my eyes.

The three people in attendance hooted and hollered, making me laugh and feel accepted. Giggling, I couldn't ignore how lighter I felt from the simple act of engaging with others.

"All done," Roxie said.

I looked down, tilting my head as I tried to see it.

"It's not gonna look pretty for a few days," she said, seeing my face. After some instructions on how to care for it and to avoid any more swimming for a month, I was sent on my way with several well wishes and hugs.

Feeling like a new woman, I strutted out of the tattoo shop in my overpriced wedding dress, intent on continuing my streak of decision-making.

Smacking into a well-dressed woman around the corner instantly threw it all into question as everything tilted on its axis.

"Mom?!"

"Blake! There you are," she shrieked, wrapping her arms around me like I'd been kidnapped for over forty-eight hours, and the police had told her to give up hope.

"*Mom*, what are you doing here?" I asked into her neck where I was currently being suffocated.

"What am *I* doing here? I think the better question

is, what are *you* doing here?" She pulled back, her eyes wide with panic as her words tumbled over one another. "You run away from your wedding, go radio silent, and then I get a ping on your card that you're at a tattoo shop, of all places! I swore to your father that it couldn't be you. No, not *our* Blake. She wouldn't risk her health and well-being for a tattoo. No, someone must've stolen her card and was using it."

She shook her head back and forth as she continued to monologue her dramatization, her hands gripping my arms like she feared I'd disappear if she let go.

"Your father said to leave you alone, that if you ran away from the altar, it meant you needed space, and I was being my usual overbearing self. But I couldn't take the chance it wasn't some degenerate using your card since it's the first clue I've gotten to your whereabouts since you went MIA."

Shame coated me at her words for making them worry and the fact my parents still provided for me and therefore had access to my bank cards. I hadn't meant to cause my family distress as I sought out choices I could make for myself, but they had, and that was on me for not taking the time to reach out.

I often hated how much they hovered, but I knew it was justified. I had been sick and almost died. That left a mark on a family and child. Though sometimes, it felt almost worse to survive, but that was a belief I'd never utter aloud. At least, not to the people who'd also gone through it. It was a secret shame I wore like a ten-pound weight.

"I'm sorry, Mom. Things got a bit overwhelming, and I just needed some time to think."

She sucked in a breath, nodding as she finally let go of my arms. Her hands moved to my face, smoothing them over my cheeks as she took in my outfit. "I don't think that was quite the look the designer had in mind for this dress, BB," she teased, showing me the fun side of my mom. Not the one obsessed with my wedding, but the mom who would take me out for ice cream and get my nails done when we were having a bad day.

"I dunno. I think it's much improved," I joked, twisting and turning as I pretended to show it off.

She grimaced but didn't comment, taking my hand in hers as she turned and walked to where she'd parked. I guess my self-journey and reckless decision-making were over for the time being.

"I kinda took over, didn't I?" she asked, regret etched on her face, her similar blue eyes flashing with guilt.

"Yeah." I sighed, stopping our trek. "I should've said something from the start, but I could tell how much everyone else wanted it. I thought, maybe if I went along with it, then I'd eventually want it too."

"Oh, BB. I'm sorry if I made you feel like you had to marry Brandon."

Her words soothed something in me, and I was glad we were having this talk. It was long overdue.

"I kept pinching myself during the proposal, waiting to wake up from the nightmare," I admitted.

She chuckled, then grimaced. "I did try to stop him

from that particular method. He's a nice boy, if not a little boring. I thought you could've had a beautiful life together, but I always wondered if he was just incredible in bed or something."

"Mother!" I gasped.

"What? Sex is an important part of a marriage, honey. Your father and I had our differences, but we never had any issues in the bedroom department."

"Ew, gross! Stop. I don't want to hear this." I covered my ears as she laughed, the mom I recognized surfacing.

"Oh, come on. I'm not that out of touch. I know you guys were sexually active. It's okay."

"But we weren't. Brandon always said he wanted to wait until marriage. I mean, we did some things, but you know… not all the way. No home run for this gal." I tilted my thumbs back at myself as I hid my rosy cheeks.

"Ha. That's a riot."

"I'm serious, Mom. I was a virgin." As soon as I said the word, I hoped she didn't question the past tense part.

"BB, I found the condom wrapper under the bed while putting away your clothes. You don't have to lie." She sighed like I was inconveniencing her.

"I'm not, Mom. Promise. But when did you find the condom wrapper?" I asked, a cold sweat breaking out.

She really looked at me then, finally getting the hint I wasn't lying to her. "A couple of months ago. You sure it wasn't yours?"

"Considering we never had sex. Yeah. It wasn't mine."

"Oh." Her eyes widened, and we both stood there stunned. I had no idea if Brandon had cheated on me or if someone else had sex in my bedroom. I didn't know which option I preferred.

"Well. What did you see in him then, honey, if the sex wasn't out of this world?" she asked, breaking up the tense moment.

My mouth dropped open, and a giggle escaped as hysteria caught up to me. "I have no clue. I asked myself the same question yesterday, and all I could come up with was he had a cute dimple and was nice. When I realized that, I knew I couldn't build a life off of it."

"Oh, thank god. I always wondered why you wanted to be B. Cupley."

I shook my head, wiping my eyes as tears fell from laughing so hard. "I hadn't ever thought of it until yesterday. Mom, if you thought he was boring, why did you pick out the wedding topper that you did? *That* I don't get."

She reared back like I'd struck her. Okay, I guess Mom was really sensitive about cake toppers.

"You thought *I* picked it out?" she gasped, and I wrinkled my brow in confusion.

"You didn't?"

She shook her head no.

"Then who?"

"Brandon."

At that, we both giggled at how he apparently saw the two of us. Holy hell, I couldn't believe I almost married a guy who saw me as a pre-makeover 'Sandy.' Nothing against the character, but it wasn't me. At least not anymore.

Hawk had been right. I was more of a Frenchie.

"I never wanted to say this," Mom admitted as she wrapped her arm in mine as we continued our walk, "but his mother was atrocious. I was not looking forward to sharing grandchildren with that woman. She would be the type to go behind your back and do things you asked her not to." She shuddered, clearly not a fan of Brandon's mother.

As we neared the car, I felt an overwhelming sense of motherly love between us and realized how much I needed my mom. This version, at least.

"I lost my virginity to Hawk last night and then pushed him away after Bryce found us together by lying that it meant nothing. Then I ran out of there like a runaway bride, this time with actual tears because it hurt worse to walk away from him than it had Brandon. Then I got a tattoo because I feel like I never get to make my own choices, and I just wanted to live instead of hiding!"

I had to give it to my mother; she took it all in stride.

Her eyes widened at my word vomit. But instead of screaming at me in outrage or even telling me how ridiculous and irresponsible I'd been, she pulled me into another hug, this one soft and reassuring as she patted my back. The tears and sobs came, and I drenched her coat, but she held onto me, rocking back and forth as I exorcised my demons through tears.

"I think this is partly my fault," she said, drawing back once the hiccups had slowed. "When you got sick, I overcompensated. I kept you tucked away, so worried I'd lose you. We got so used to the roles that we didn't know how to break free from them, even when you became an adult. If I'd listened to you during the wedding planning instead of focusing on how happy I was to see you as a bride, I would've realized how checked out you were. I'm sorry, BB."

"It's okay, Mom. I didn't know how to say no. I didn't want to disappoint you."

"You could never disappoint me, sweetie. You're my miracle."

Fresh tears fell, but I felt lighter.

"What do you need? Did you use protection? Do we need to go to the pharmacy?"

I shook my head and gave her a soft smile. "No. Hawk used protection."

She sighed in relief. "I knew I always liked that boy. He treated you okay?"

"Yeah, Mom. He did. He was amazing, and I think I could love him, but I can't do that to Bry."

"Your brother loves you both. He might not be able to accept it now but don't give up on him. He always does like to wait until a full count to swing."

She kept petting my hair, stroking it as we spoke. It was soothing and comforting, something I'd desperately been needing.

"A small part of me kept hoping he'd stop me and tell Bryce that he loved me too. But he didn't. Even though I know I started it by saying it meant nothing, I wanted him to prove me wrong in some epic romantic gesture. But he just went along with it. He let me break both of our hearts. Why?"

"Rejection is a hard thing to swallow for anyone, BB, and you know how hard it's been for him since Libby died. Just give him time."

Sucking in a breath, I knew my mom was right. But I couldn't wait around for some romantic gesture or for Hawk to save me from the mess I made. Actions had consequences, and I'd set us on this path. It was time I rescued myself.

"How much of a mess did I make?" I asked, picking at my nails or what was left of them.

"Nothing your father's PR team can't handle. Don't worry about that. You did the right thing."

"Hawk and I broke into the reception and stole food and cake, by the way. It was delicious. You did a great job."

Mom laughed, asking me how we managed it, and I regaled her with the fork-brandishing moment.

"Oh, BB, I can just picture it. My fierce little warrior princess."

"Thanks, though I don't feel much like a warrior princess, much less a fierce one," I admitted, dropping my eyes. "I hate my job. I still live at home and just left my fiance at the altar. It's not really all that great in my corner right now."

"I have an idea, but I want you to think about it and not do it just because I'm suggesting it," she said, holding my eyes until I nodded in agreement. "Aunt Lola has always wanted you to visit. This could be the perfect opportunity. You already have time off from work for the honeymoon. Go and visit her instead. Get away from everything here and see if you can find your own path."

Aunt Lola, Mom's younger sister. The wild one.

I hadn't seen her since I was little, not since she moved to Greece. "Do you think she'd be okay with that?"

"Of course. She'd love it. And there's this new wellness center she told me about. I think it could be time to see someone and figure out who you are, away from baseball and your illness."

"And you all."

She shrugged, but I could see the sadness in her eyes. It was how I knew this wasn't a ploy but a true lifeline she was giving me—a chance to break out on my own and be me without the influence of anyone else.

It felt scary. The furthest I'd ever been away from my family was an hour. I didn't know if I could go two whole weeks.

But it also sounded amazing and exhilarating. My heart thumped in my chest at the thought of exploring myself and talking to someone who didn't know me. I'd always wanted to do therapy, but something always stopped me.

"It's not running away?" I asked, biting my lip.

"What's your father always say about running the bases?" she asked, lifting a brow.

I sighed and nodded. "You gotta know when to steal and when to retreat."

"Exactly. I think this is the perfect time to retreat and let your heart heal."

I sucked in a deep breath as I thought it over and realized she was right.

"Help me pack?"

My mom smiled and hugged me, kissing me on the cheek as she nodded. And just like that, I was heading off to prepare for a trip.

Blake

TEN

PEOPLE ZOOMED past me in a rush as I ambled toward the security line. With my ticket in hand, I peered around at the other travelers, watching as loved ones said goodbye before dashing into the line, eager to continue their journey. Mothers with small children already looked stressed as they dragged their charges along, a collection of bags and tickets strapped to them. Businessmen and women sped off without a backward glance, so accustomed to traveling they efficiently went through the practiced motions.

"You sure this is what you want to do, BB?" Bryce asked, drawing my attention back to him. After scolding me for disappearing from the hotel room without leaving even a note, he insisted on bringing me. He was wrong on that front—I'd left the bee pin next to the bed for Hawk as some weird memento, perhaps— but I didn't correct him. As it was, I wasn't ready to say goodbye yet, so I'd easily agreed to his terms.

Bryce's brows were drawn as he stared at me, waiting for a response. The worry creases around his mouth and eyes were on full display as he watched me. I squeezed his hand, taking comfort in his touch.

"I think I need to, Bryce. It's time."

Sighing, he accepted my answer and pulled me into his arms for a hug. I clutched onto him, needing one last familiar thing before I left. He kissed my hair before drawing back, wiping at his eyes.

"Call me when you land, and I'll be here to pick you up in two weeks."

"But training camp," I started, stopping when he gave me a look.

"I'll be here, Blanket. Promise. I love you more than free Wi-Fi."

"Love you more than chocolate milk," I said back, our way of saying we loved one another since child-hood. "Try not to get into any fights while I'm gone," I teased.

"No promises there. If Olson opens his pretty boy mouth, I might have to shut it."

"And you wonder why Hawk is your only friend."

"I have others," he protested, making me chuckle.

"Try not to break too many hearts. I won't be here to console all the girls when they realize you're not going to propose."

"If you're going to give me all these rules, I think you should just stay. It's easier for me." He laughed.

"Speaking of, Mom said she found a condom

wrapper under my bed. Did you take one of your hookups into *my* room?" I narrowed my eyes.

"And on that note, it's time for you to go, sister dearest." He took my shoulders and pushed me toward the line. I let him, but I didn't miss how his cheeks had tinted pink. Bryce had his own place, so I didn't know why he needed to hook up in my room, but there were some crazy cleat chasers and ball girls out there.

Waving goodbye, I contemplated the absurdity of the terms "cleat chaser" and "ball girl" as I stood in line. I didn't know which was worse: the fact there were terms for girls who sought out baseball players to sleep with or that baseball players were placed on a scoring card, and sleeping with them gave someone status or clout.

Maybe because I'd grown up around professional players my whole life and knew them on a first-name basis, but I didn't see the appeal. They were just guys with bigger egos who were on the road for half of the year. If anything, I'd always run far away from dating baseball players. It had to be why I'd stayed with Brandon for so long. He was so far outside of a baseball player that he'd seemed safe, which was probably the wrong reason to date someone.

After successfully separating my liquids, electronics, and shoes into different bins, I passed through security and collected my carry-on. People rushed off in every direction, eager to make their flights as I took a minute to get my bearings. In perfect Blake fashion, I'd arrived four hours early for my flight, so I had plenty of time to kill.

It wasn't even that I'd been worried about missing it. But the longer I sat at home, the easier it was to back out. My fear and anxiety had overwhelmed me, and I was halfway to convincing myself it wasn't a big deal and I should just stay home.

But it wasn't true. I *needed* to do this.

Wandering through the terminal, I stopped at a newsstand to grab snacks and entertainment for the flight. Browsing through the magazines, I moved on to the book stands. Reaching for one with a blue cover, my hand collided with another—a very male hand.

"Oh, sorry," I stammered, jumping back and spinning toward the person the hand belonged to.

Gray eyes smiled at me, and I blinked to ensure I wasn't hallucinating. But nope, his eyes were smiling. Somehow.

"Have you read that one?" the owner of the gray smiling eyes asked. He was about a head and a half taller than me, stocky with solid muscles. Brown hair poked out of the side of a backward cap, showcasing his eyes, kind smile, and a chin dotted with stubble. He was a few years younger than me, maybe a senior in college, if his sweatshirt was anything to go by.

It took a minute for my brain to process that he'd asked me a question, too busy cataloging his features.

I cleared my throat and shook my head. "No, I haven't. It just looked interesting. You?"

"Yeah. It's really good. One of my favorites." He

smiled, my stomach warming up under his gaze. He blinked as he rolled those hypnotizing eyes over me, taking me in now. I had on black leggings, a flowy crop top, and my hot pink high tops. Not really an outfit to grab attention, but picked for comfort.

But the way his eyes lingered, it didn't seem like he minded.

"You should take it then," I offered when I noticed there was only one left. He grinned again, the look making him adorably boyish. I had the sudden need to curl up in his lap while he read to me.

"No, I insist. I need to branch out anyway and read new things. Just sometimes, it's nice to re-read a favorite. It's like a warm cup of hot chocolate."

He plucked another paperback off the shelf and the one we'd been reaching for. He handed me the blue one and gave me one last grin before he headed to the register.

"Thanks," I whispered, tingles racing up my arm from where he'd touched my hand. By the time I got my bearings and turned to ask his name, he was already gone.

"You're not engaged anymore, girl. If you see a cute guy, you can ask his name," I whispered to myself, making the woman behind me chuckle.

Cheeks reddening, I quickly grabbed some snacks and paid for my things, wondering if I would be able to make it on my own. As of right now, the results were hazy.

For the next two hours, I roamed the airport,

hopping into shops and buying things I saw. I couldn't remember the last time I'd been shopping by myself, and for that alone, the novelty of it felt exciting. I probably didn't need the embellished eye mask or the quirky pillow that wrapped around my bag, but I'd have fun with them.

Leaving the store, I turned toward my gate when someone rammed into me, knocking me to the ground and spilling my purchases everywhere. My butt hit the floor, and I winced as I landed, trying to figure out what had just happened.

A guy cursed across from me as he bent down on one knee, rubbing a scuff off his pristine white tennis shoes. He expelled some creative ones, sighing when the black mark wouldn't come out.

"Try some baking soda," I offered, reaching for my bag. He looked up at my comment, his eyes widening at my predicament.

"Oh, shit. They got you good," he said, abandoning his shoe to help me collect my belongings. He picked up one of my new purchases, his lips quirking up into a smile as he placed it into the bag, not saying anything. I knew what it looked like, and as his cheeks heated and his brown eyes flicked up to me, it was clear what he thought it was.

"It's not what it looks like," I defended, taking the oblong-shaped object and stuffing it into my bag.

He lifted his hands in surrender, smiling as he stared at me. "No judgment."

I rolled my eyes, fighting the blush that wanted to

stain my cheeks. Once everything was back in, I was surprised to find his offered hand to help me stand.

"Thanks," I said as he easily pulled me up like I was a feather, the muscles flexing in his forearm. I peered up and up at him, swallowing as I took in his height. He had to be well over six feet, making him several heads taller than me. His rich brown eyes danced as he gave me a cocky smile, one I was sure worked on whoever he directed it at.

He had shaggy brown hair with curls that flew all over the place in a messy way. It made his face softer, making him more approachable. He had the body of a fuckboy, all muscles and tanned, but with his sweet nature and eager attitude to help, I didn't think he actually was.

"It's a massager," I defended, needing to prove my point further.

"Uh-huh." He smiled wider and winked, sucking the breath right out of me.

Oh, this boy was dangerous.

He made me feel like I'd known him forever as he smiled down at me with his warm eyes made of honey.

"I'm—" His words were cut off as someone yelled for him behind me.

"TJ! The plane's boarding now. Coach will kill us if we miss it."

He grimaced and gave me a nod and a pat on my shoulder before he took off at a run. I turned and watched him go, not even a little bit embarrassed watching how nice his butt looked as it flexed in his pants.

My phone vibrated, pulling me from his hypnotic spell and alerting me to head to the gate. With everything back securely in my bag, I made my way to my B23, careful not to be plowed over by any other passersby this time.

It wasn't until I was sitting in my seat next to a sweet old lady that I realized it was two for two in cute guys I'd forgotten to flirt with. Not that I'd ever see either of them again. And based on the fact one was in college and the other an athlete, they weren't guys I should be interested in anyway.

But the fact remained, I needed more practice. Then I could possibly get Hawk out of my mind and heart.

"Aunt Lola, I'm not sure about this," I panted as I attempted to balance on my head. I'd never felt more like an unbalanced klutz than I did attempting to do yoga with my aunt.

"Ssh, Bee. You need to focus," she said, her legs up straight as her core muscles kept her perfectly balanced on her head.

Nope. I wasn't jealous of my forty-year-old aunt.

Giving up, I fell over and wiped the sweat from my brow, and sucked in enough air to calm my lungs.

The past two weeks here had been exactly what I

needed. My aunt lived in this hip region in Greece that catered to mindfulness retreats and anyone looking to reset and recharge. It was a whole wellness area that had yoga, massages, and counseling; it was the perfect self-care oasis. Everything felt alive here, from the food to the people, and even the atmosphere, that it was impossible to wallow in self-pity.

Though, once the jetlag and homesickness hit, I'd tried.

Aunt Lola poured a bucket of cold water on me and then smacked me with leaves, telling me it was with love. I didn't know about the love part, but at least it had worked to get me out of bed.

Once I'd quit fighting the place, I fell in love with it. Aunt Lola had amazing friends who had all taken me under their wings, showing me new experiences every day. It was the first year I hadn't hated my birthday either, blowing out candles on a huge cake my new friends had made.

Each day was a new adventure. I hiked to ancient ruins, tried new foods I'd never heard of, and even got a makeover. That had been Emory's idea, the daughter of Aunt Lola's partner, Calliope. Emory was a year older than me, and we'd become instant friends. Having more than just my parents and Bryce to talk to felt nice.

Somewhere between running away from Emerald Stadium and getting on that plane, I realized I only had a handful of numbers in my phone—and most were doctors.

I was twenty-five with no social life. Even I had to admit it was pathetic.

But two weeks away and that had changed.

Surprisingly, baseball was not the number one subject of conversation here, and going without it for two weeks made me miss it. I'd even talked to the therapist about it, and she was helping me find a new way to experience the sport. I wanted to feel like I belonged in my family, but not like it was the only thing that mattered.

It was a relief to voice that and be validated and heard.

Therapy had been precisely what I needed. I'd done four sessions so far and had one more before I left tomorrow. There was still so much to unpack with my illness and family that I actually regretted having to leave. I never thought I'd be able to be away this long, much less not be eager to return home.

"Lake!" Emory yelled as she rushed into the yoga room. That had been one other thing that had changed. Everyone called me Bee or Lake here, depending on their age. The older crowd tended to use the more affectionate Bee, while the people my age liked the edgier Lake, stating it fit my new look.

Pink strands stuck to my sweaty forehead, and I swiped them out of my face as I turned to my new friend. She held a big envelope in her hand, a massive smile on her face as she stared at me, practically vibrating on the spot.

"Is that it?" I asked, gasping as I quickly stood.

"I can't open it. Will you?" she pleaded, her hands trembling.

Nodding, I took the thick cardstock and flicked it open. The invitation was ornate, and I smiled as I read it out.

"Emory Samaras, you've been cordially invited to attend this year's Fête de la Fraise as a featured pâtisserie. Please see the enclosed itinerary for more details."

I looked up, and we both screamed as we jumped up and down, clutching one another.

"I knew you'd get invited," I said, a twinge of sadness that I wouldn't be here to support her hitting me.

"I mean, I hoped. But I never believed," she gushed, her accent thick with emotion. "You should come with me!" she squealed, her eyes lighting up.

"What? No. I couldn't. I'm supposed to head back tomorrow." I shook my head, frowning at my new best friend.

"But do you have to? Not to be brash, but what's waiting for you there? You don't want to work in business. You're no longer engaged, and the rest of your family is preoccupied with baseball. Tell me I'm not wrong?" She lifted her brow and crossed her arms, daring me to contradict her.

I hated how right she was. I didn't have anything to return to, and while this trip had been exactly what I needed, it only highlighted how dull and lonely my life in Ohio was.

Not to mention the niggling doubt that the second I stepped foot back in America, I'd return to the no-boundaries, no-backbone, and no-personality Blake I'd become.

But staying here… could I really do that?

Thankfully, Aunt Lola finished her yoga and joined our huddle, gushing and hugging Emory as they both cried in Greek.

Believe me; it was a whole thing.

The rest of the night, as I packed my suitcase to leave the next day, I couldn't shake the question… Could I stay longer?

"How are you feeling about returning home?" Delia, my therapist, asked me.

"Nervous. I'm worried I haven't changed enough," I admitted, picking my nails, something I hadn't done in two weeks.

"What do you feel would be enough?" she asked, redirecting the question back to me.

"I guess I still don't know who I am. I might have a tattoo and pink hair now, but on the inside, I still feel like that girl who's afraid of burdening people, who feels she needs to be constantly grateful for being alive."

"The gratitude shackles."

"Yes, exactly. I don't think I've lost them yet. I feel stronger in many ways and know I can't run away forever. The seventh inning stretch can only last so long." I smiled, laughing at how even when I was on my own, baseball still snuck in.

It felt nice, though. Like using a secret language I had with my family. Which instantly made me think of Dad and his baseball theories and wondering if there was one for this situation. I'd assumed life had thrown me a curveball, but perhaps it had been a changeup all along.

Was I striking out because I'd been reading the pitch wrong the whole time?

"What did you just think about?" Delia asked, bringing me out of my head.

"My dad has this theory that baseball can solve any problem. Either by attending a game, hitting a few balls, or the rules themselves. I've been thinking I had to swing at each option presented to me without focusing on everything else around me and waiting for the perfect pitch."

"It sounds like you've found some solace in your dad's theories; a bit of comfort?"

"Yeah. I think I have."

"And what did you discover? You had a smile on your face, and I watched your whole body relax immediately as you realized something."

Her question made me blink, not having known that much had been going on in my body language. "I realized I was returning home because that was the plan. I had two weeks off from work, and that's my ticket's return date."

"But?" she asked, smiling at me, knowing I'd gained some insight.

"But..." I grinned. "Just because that's what is expected doesn't mean I have to do it."

Damn, that felt good to say out loud.

"What is it you want to do?"

I smiled with my whole face, not even having to dig deep for the answer this time. "No, I want to stay. I like who I'm becoming here, and I'm not ready to stop that growth yet. I have enough savings to stay longer, and if my job won't hold my position, I'll find something else. It's not like I enjoy it, anyway. Emory has asked me to join her while she's at Fête de la Fraise, and that sounds a lot more fun than counting numbers."

"And what about this? Do you want to continue our work?"

"Definitely. We're just at the tip of the iceberg, Doc."

She chuckled, her eyes soft as she looked at me. "Shall we role-play telling your parents, then?"

I nodded vigorously with my eyes wide, making her laugh. We both knew despite my desire to stay and feeling it was best for me, I'd still struggle to tell my parents, especially if they protested to any degree.

Baby steps. I just had to keep moving forward. One base at a time, as Dad said.

As the session ended, Delia stood and walked over to her bookcase. She picked up an old film camera with a purple strap that had seen better days.

"I uncovered this camera over the weekend while cleaning out some boxes. It's been well-loved, but it still functions. I'd like for you to take it and use it as a homework exercise."

"You want me to take pictures?" I asked, my forehead creasing. It seemed like an odd request.

"Yes, and no. I want you to take pictures of things that make you smile. Things that make you sad. Things that move you in any way. Find the beauty in the mundane, in the brokenness. Then I'll show you how to develop the film. If you hate it after a few tries, then we can try something new. But I have a feeling you might like seeing things from a different perspective."

Taking the camera into my hands, I felt a sense of rightness as I held it. Excitement to take pictures and learn a new skill bubbled inside me, eclipsing the fear of telling my parents I wasn't leaving today.

I didn't know if that was Delia's intention, but I had a feeling she didn't do or say anything without reason.

With the camera clutched in my grasp, I headed out of her office with my shoulders back, head up, and determination in my steps. It was time for me to step up to the plate. I might swing and miss, or I might hit it out of the park.

But I'd never know until I tried.

It was rally cap time.

Blake

EPILOGUE

HANGING up the last photo to dry, I stepped back and gazed at the images as they materialized on the film. The day Delia gave me her old camera, a passion unfurled within me. Neither of us had known the significance of that moment at that time, but it was one I'd be forever grateful for.

I'd upgraded to a DSLR camera that I used for most things, but there was something therapeutic and organic about developing film that I enjoyed. I pulled out that old camera—now with a new sunflower strap —at least once a week and took stock of the things around me.

Delia had been right about how much I enjoyed seeing things from a different perspective. It opened my eyes to a whole new world, where I saw the entire frame and not just the plays in front of me.

Baseball and photography metaphor for the win.

Stepping out of the darkroom—a converted closet that Aunt Lola and Calliope had made for me—I walked to the sliding door. The weather here was always perfect, and I took a deep breath of the salty air as it blew in off the coast. Wind chimes jingled in the background, and I rested back in the hammock swing to stare at the sky. Life was so peaceful here.

I hadn't meant to stay in Greece this long, but each time I thought about returning to Ohio, I'd get a pit in the bottom of my stomach and find some excuse to stay.

The first year was to finish therapy and explore the world around me, which my parents had accepted without too much fuss. I went with Emory to Paris and met the most fascinating individuals. We danced, laughed, and kissed a few boys from Paris to Madrid, and I'd never felt so carefree.

There was a little health scare midway through that year, and my parents almost demanded I return home, but Aunt Lola had calmed them down, and I showed myself I could be sick without falling back into my "helpless" pattern.

That was one of those things I'd learned in therapy, too. Along with my gratitude shackles, I believed that people only wanted to be around me when they could take care of me. This led to me giving control of my life and letting everyone else make the decisions for me, always rescuing me.

I'd come to accept it was a main component of why I'd dated Brandon. Not only had my mom adored him, but he was a natural leader. He replaced my parents by making decisions for me, allowing me never to think for myself or be responsible. I realized how easily I could be manipulated if I continued on that path, leading me to darker and more dangerous territory. I was grateful that even though Brandon wasn't the guy for me, he'd been a good man. A little boring, perhaps, but he hadn't been abusive or controlling. And I'd forgiven him for the whole cake topper thing.

There was a moment in year two when I nearly caved. Hawk was injured, ending his baseball career, and I ached to console him, to make sure he was okay. But my heart didn't feel strong enough yet, so I sent him care packages and got updates from Bryce when I could. We were still radio silent, not even a text in two years, but I hoped he knew I cared.

After his recovery, Dad offered him a coaching job with the Yellowjackets, and he'd taken it, putting him and Bryce back on the same team again. I was happy for him, even if it still hurt to think about the chance we never got.

A butterfly landed on my knee, tickling the skin and distracting me from memory road. Smiling, I reached for my phone to snap it. Uploading it to my social media account, I scrolled through all the images I'd added over the years, landing on a picture of a cute guy helping a little girl kick a ball—the reason I'd stayed the next year.

I'd been offered a position taking pictures for the local sports teams, and I hadn't wanted to leave yet. I enjoyed finding new ways to use a skill I was passionate about. There might've also been the hot coach I was dating that influenced my decision. It didn't last long, but it was nice to date someone that wasn't Brandon. And while the sex had been nice, it was nowhere near my time with Hawk, and I wondered if I'd been reverse cursed—never to experience an orgasm not by my own hands again.

I'd thought about returning after my contract ended and my relationship fluttered out, but I heard through the gossip grapevine that Hawk was seeing someone, and the pain that lanced my heart was so intense that I knew I still couldn't face him. Again, I was glad he was moving forward in his life, but it still hurt to know I wouldn't be in it.

The patio door opened, and I lazily turned my head toward the sound. Emory bounded over, her light brown hair flying around her. She had on one of the shirts I'd made her that said, "Sunshine mixed with a little hurricane." Nothing had ever seemed more perfect than that statement. That had been another therapy project I'd uncovered. Delia had encouraged me to expand my pins into shirts, giving me something to focus on and finding funny ways to say the things I was often too bashful to utter.

Emory smiled when she spotted me in the hammock and raced over to join me, jostling me as she made herself comfortable.

"Lake, my beautiful friend, how are you today?" Emory beamed, crossing one long leg over the other,

her tan skin on display. She was effortlessly beautiful, a true free spirit, and a lover of anything fun.

"I'm good. Just finished developing that last roll of film."

"Oh, I can't wait to see your newest masterpieces. Are you putting any of them up in the gallery?"

At the end of last year, I submitted a photo to a contest per Emory's insistence and was completely surprised when I won. A gallery owner had seen my image and contacted me, interested in buying prints to showcase. It felt weird to sell my photos, though. They were a part of me, and it was odd to think they'd be out there in the world on other people's walls.

Emory said I had a case of imposter syndrome and needed to embrace my talent. So I sucked it up and submitted a few, completely flabbergasted when they sold within a week. The owner told me to send whatever I had whenever, and they would showcase them. It was nice, but I enjoyed doing sports photography the most.

It had taken me a while to accept it, but once I did, I knew it was how I could relate to my family and do something I loved. I wasn't sure what it would look like long-term, but I had faith there was a way.

But in the meantime, it was a stream of revenue I couldn't ignore, especially after making a point to not depend on my parents anymore and to make it on my own. It hadn't always been easy, but I'd learned a lot about budgeting and stretching a euro until my unicorn job appeared.

"Yeah. Angelica has called and texted me daily, asking if I had anything new."

"You're so in demand, and you don't even care. I love it." She giggled, shaking the hammock as she smacked my leg.

My phone rang, and my brother's photo popped up on the screen before I could reply to her.

"Ooh, is that Brycey-boo?" Emory hummed, waggling her eyebrows like a loon as she stared at the photo that had popped up.

They'd met when Bryce had visited in the off-season. I wasn't certain, but it seemed like something had happened between them, but neither of them would admit to anything. It was one of those things where it felt better not to ask. Not to mention that since her mom and our aunt were married, it made us some weird form of cousins. Cousin-adjacent?

Tapping the accept button, I lifted the phone to my ear and gave Emory a look to be quiet.

"Hey, Bry. How's it going?"

"Prepare to be blown away, Sis." I swallowed, nerves swirling in my stomach. It was the end of March, the time of year when everyone tried to convince me to return home before baseball season started. Except Ohio wasn't really my home anymore. But I knew I couldn't stay here forever. If anything, I was a nomad looking for my Hobbit hut.

"Hmm, that's a big promise, Bro." I could almost feel him smile as he prepared to launch into his Power-Point presentation.

"Oh, but it is. I found your unicorn job."

My breath hitched, and I sat up, almost rolling Emory out of the hammock. She squeaked and laughed as she righted herself, and I mouthed "sorry" to her.

"Is that Emory?" Bryce asked, his voice sounding higher.

"Yep. She's in the hammock with me."

"Oh. Cool. Cool. Cool."

Never had I heard my calm and collected brother so flustered. *Interesting*.

"So, unicorn?" I asked, reminding my brother what he had called about.

"Right. So, I don't know if you've been watching the different sports teams blow up on LiveIt or not over there, but their social media followers have tripled as they've been interacting with the fans and pulling in Book-It."

"Book-It," I said, but it came out as more of a question, wondering if he was making shit up. LiveIt wasn't a thing here.

"Yes, exactly," he responded excitedly, missing that I hadn't known what he was talking about. "And then the Banana Pajamas launched into the stratosphere on there. Sports teams are changing how they interact with fans and bringing a new crowd to the games. It's not just arrival photos and press conferences anymore. It's so much more," he gushed, his excitement building as he spoke.

I had to admit; it did sound interesting and fun.

"What does this have to do with me and my unicorn job?" I asked, too nervous to hope yet.

"I convinced Dad that the Yellowjackets needed that. We need to boost our team image, get more fans in the stands, and get our players' names out there. It's easier for the pro guys, but in the Minors, you're almost forgotten."

He didn't outright say it, but I could hear the genuine sadness in his voice, the fear and hurt he felt at being stuck on the Yellowjackets for the past three years. His window of playing in the Majors was closing, and he wanted to boost his chance of getting noticed.

"What did he say?" I asked, curious as to where I fit in this. I knew they already had a social media person, a team photographer, and a videographer, so it wasn't like it was something open he could offer me.

"He was all for it. Especially when I said that you should be the one to do it."

"Wait. *Me?*"

"Yes, you, Blanket. It's time you came home." His smile was there again in his voice, hitting a wave of homesickness I hadn't felt in years. Could it be that easy? Just go home?

"But… I thought those roles were filled," I stuttered, unwilling to believe it was that simple.

"Technically, yes. But Rachel is going on maternity leave, and Sanders broke his pelvis. Larry will still be doing the videography of the games, but the other two spots have a temporary vacancy. I pitched the idea that you could fill in for both, and if it worked, we could create a position primarily for TikTok, someone who would focus only on content for it. I know it sounds like a lot right now. You'd be traveling with the team and spending most of your days with them… with me."

How could you say no to your brother when he spelled it out like that?

"Hmm, what's the pay?" I countered a giddiness that I might have found the perfect job finally. "If I have to be around you and a bunch of smelly baseball players, then it better be good."

"Ha ha." But when Bryce told me the starting salary, I almost choked on my own saliva.

"Shut. Up."

"I know it's not great," he started, misunderstanding, and I wanted to shake him for thinking 50K a season, with bonuses and travel expenses paid, wasn't that great. I got that he was a professional baseball player, and his signing bonus alone with the Blue Devils had been in the millions. And even though he was playing in the Minors now, he still got paid out of his Majors' contract. But for most people, that was a dream salary. Considering I'd been living off of less than that for three years combined, it was a massive jump in income for me.

"When do you need me back?" I asked, flitting my eyes over to Emory. She patted my leg and gave me a knowing smile. We always knew I'd leave one day, but it didn't make it any easier to say goodbye. She'd become the best friend and sister I'd always wanted. Though, I wouldn't tell Bryce that. But there were some things you couldn't tell your brother, no matter how close you were.

"In three days. Opening day is right around the corner."

I could hear the grimace in his voice as the bottom fell out of me. *Three days.*

Three days to say goodbye to a family and life I'd carved for myself.

Three days to mentally prepare to return home, determined not to be the same boneless Blake.

Three days to convince myself that seeing Hawk again wouldn't rip out my heart. Especially since he'd moved on.

"Okay. I'll do it. I'm coming home."

The cleat retreat was officially over, and there were no more excuses to stay away. It was time to start the next inning of my life.

Yellowjackets, get ready because this Bee is coming for you.

To be continued in The Pitch Slap

AFTERWORD

Are you ready to dive into this new world? Blake has a rocky start, but I'm hoping you'll come to love her sassy side as she grows into it. Hawk is the book-boyfriend dreams are made of, but it's not going to go smoothly at first as these two try to find their way back. Thankfully, Blake will have Luke, Tucker, and Graham to keep her busy. Did you catch their mentions?

This series will be interconnected standalones with different relationship types. Blake's book will be why-choose with bi-awakening themes, Bryce's book will be ménage, and Ledger's book will be MM. All books will have LGBTQ+ characters in them.

There's a lot planned for Beauty and the Cleats, so I hope you fall in love with them just as much as I have.

Now, on to the acknowledgements.

First, I want to thank my husband for his support of my writing. He gives me the space to spend hours at my computer, understands when not to interrupt me, and helps me brainstorm names and titles. And after this last book signing, he earned his book husband title by going above and beyond. So, thank you, babe, you're the best!

Emma, you're my rock and the best cheerleader. Thank you for everything.

Heather, otherwise known as Best Hype Woman, thank you for keeping me straight on the names and fact-checking.

Melanie and Megan, thank you both for giving me your feedback and sports knowledge.

Lindsay, thank you so much for powering through and helping me meet my deadlines.

Seriously, thank you all for your love and support. You're my rockstars!

Emma Smith, thank you for this beautiful photo you took of Kaylee. She makes a great Blake.

To my ARC readers and Street team, and all the people who pick up this book, thank you for giving a new world of mine a chance. Now, while you wait for The Pitch Slap, check out the rest of my books and find something new to love.

ALSO BY KRIS BUTLER

For the most up-to-date look at my releases. Check out all my books here: https://authorkrisbutler.com/my-books

BEAUTY AND THE CLEATS

#baseball #standalone series #heartfelt

The Cleat Retreat (Blake's prequel)

The Pitch Slap (Blake's book, MMFMM)

No Balking Way (Bryce's book, MMF)

Whiff it Real Good (Ledger's book, MM)

LUX BRUMALIS (COMPLETED)

#hockey #girlboss #nonbinary sibling

3 guys, no MM

Penalty Box

Dead Lift

Breakaway

THE COUNCIL SERIES (COMPLETED)

#figure skating #secret past #dark elements

7 guys, lots of MM with bi-awakening

Damaged Dreams

Shattered Secrets

Fractured Futures

Bosh Bells & Epic Fails

The Council Boxset

THE ORDER DUET (COUNCIL SPINOFF)

#secret agency #spy + hacker games #fashionista

4 guys, light MM (in book 2 at the end, and bonus)

Stiletto Sins

Lipstick Lies

The Order Duet Omnibus

DRESSED TO KILL SHARED WORLD (STANDALONE)

#female assassin #quirky & curvy #twins

4 guys, no MM

Raven

F*CK STEAL KILL (STANDALONE)

#morally gray #bestie unalivers #sassy

3 guys, biawakening, (FF in Joy's chapter)

F*ck Steal Kill

DARK CONFESSIONS (COMPLETED)

#mafia #therapist #foster kids + dogs #tattoos

5 guys with MM

Dangerous Truths

Dangerous Lies

Dangerous Vows

Reckless (Cami's Novella)

Relentless (Nat's Novella)

Dangerous Love

TATTOOED HEARTS DUET (COMPLETED)

#tattoos #penpals #music #curvy fmc

3 guys with MM

Riddled Deceit (Part 1)

Smudged Lines (Part 2)

Open Road (Road trip Novella)

Tattooed Hearts Completed Duet

MUSIC CITY DIARIES (TATTOOED HEARTS SPIN-OFF)

#motorcycle club #age gap #TW #cam girl

4 guys, no MM

Beautiful Agony

Beautiful Envy

VACATION ROMCOM

#romcom #social media experiment #besties

3 guys, no MM

Vibing

SINNERS FAIRYTALES (STANDALONE)

#Rapunzel retelling #dance #TW

3 guys, no MM

Pride

ABOUT THE AUTHOR

Kris Butler writes under a pen name to have some separation from her everyday life. Writing has become her second love, providing a safe place to normalize mental health through her characters. Kris enjoys writing emotional books with flawed characters, sassy heroines, and all the book boyfriends she loves to drool over. You can find her at home most nights reading with her husband and furbaby, trying to maintain her nerdy sock collection, or playing tabletop games with her friends. Kris loves to talk with readers about her books, even if it's just them yelling at her for that cliffhanger. If you enjoyed her book, please consider leaving a review. You can find her in her reader group or on social media.